"He, who has begun a good work in you, will carry it to completion till the return of Jesus Christ."

Philippians 1:6

For those who came* Book 2

LETTERS FROM KANSAS

Arlene Crocker-Longnickel

Cover designed by Scott Kosarich
Author's photo by Ashleigh Johnson

First printing: November 2015
Second printing: April 2017
CreateSpace.com/Amazon/Kindle

DEDICATIONS

Special thanks to my fabulous critique partners:

Denise Hoke
Paula Hilderbrand-Slater

This book was developed through your diligent and expert editing. Thank you.

Scott, for the hours that you spent with me, I will be forever grateful. Without you this book would never have been completed.

Not to forget my many friends and family who were willing to read different drafts; Gene & Angela Yates, Mary Meehan, Patti & Shiloh Risch, Paula Kigame, Gaye Hartlip, Edie Messick and Russ Hoke. Thanks to all of you.

Chris and his staff at the Fortuna Library were an invaluable help in getting my research materials.

LETTERS FROM KANSAS

PROLOGUE

A sixteen year old Bonnie Rogers sat on the attic floor alongside her mother looking into a box of old letters that belonged to her great-great Grandmother,
Margaret Reeding. Two years ago, after having read her gram's journal, she had given a report on them for her English class. The next year the journal stories were made into a play and performed by her drama class. She was now excitedly looking forward to reading some of the letters written to her Grams from friends and family who lived back in Willow Creek. This time she wanted to put everything she learned into a book.

Did the town's founder marry the San Francisco entertainer? Did Matt's love of card playing get him into trouble? Was Lydia, the beloved school teacher, meant to always be single? Did the industries newcomer, Blackie Kwasney build his fancy Golden Palace near Willow Creek? Who was the Widow Spriggs and why was she so impossibly disagreeable? And what about Sam and the newspaper he dreamed of starting?

Bonnie longed to know the answers to these questions and she hoped that the letters would tell about these people and satisfy her curiosity. Besides, she felt close to all of the people who were such an integral part of her beloved great-great Grandmother Margaret's life.

CHAPTER ONE

It was a warm summer morning: Bonnie had opened one of the small windows in the attic. The soft breeze stirred up the air and Bonnie wondered if they should move downstairs.

"Mom, do you think we should take this carton down to the living room? The dust up here can't be good for either one of us."

Her mom nodded in agreement. They each took an end of the rather good sized cardboard box and maneuvered it towards the stairs that led down to the hallway below.

As they brought the box into the living room, they joined Margaret who was sitting comfortably on the sofa. Placing the box in front of her on the low table, they began sorting through the contents.

After a few moments, Bonnie's mother excused herself saying, "I'll leave this project to the two of you. When you're finished, come into the kitchen, I'm baking some sweet rolls to go with the fresh coffee I just made."

Margaret picked up a packet of letters wrapped with a faded ribbon. Looking at Bonnie she said, "These are some letters that I felt were especially worth saving, they contain memorable events."

She handed the stack of faded letters to Bonnie. Glancing through another bundle Bonnie remarked, "Golly Grams, you've sorted these by names. It's going to be easy to follow people and events you left in Willow Creek."

Grams handed Bonnie yet another packet she had picked out of the box, "Here honey, take these, they're some of the very first letters I received."

"Thank you so much for sharing these with me Grams." Giving her a big hug, and taking the bundles of letters, Bonnie headed upstairs to her bedroom. She laid the packets on the table next to her reading chair, then returned downstairs.

When Bonnie entered the kitchen her mom and grams were already seated at the table with a cup of coffee; "Ready for a snack honey?" her mom asked. Sitting in the middle of the table was a plate of cinnamon sweet rolls.

"They smell absolutely yummy!" Bonnie walked over to the stove, poured herself a cup of coffee, and sat down. Taking a roll from the plate, she bit into it.

"Any plans for this afternoon?" her Mom asked. "I'd appreciate your doing a little shopping for me if you have time."

"Nope, no plans. I'd be glad to pick up some things for you, got a list?"

Later that evening, after dinner dishes had been put away, Bonnie excused herself and went upstairs to her room. Once settled in her chair, she turned on the small lamp that sat on the table and picked up the packets. She pulled one out from the top of the pile. This first letter had the name 'Caleb', neatly printed on it.

Miss Kitty meandered into the bedroom just then and jumped up onto Bonnie's lap. "Want to share Grams letters with me Kitty?" Lifting the kitten up to her face, Bonnie snuggled with her. "You're so soft and loveable," she murmured.

Putting Miss Kitty back on her lap Bonnie ran her hand over the kitten's back as she purred contentedly and settled down. Bonnie turned back to the letter. Carefully opening the envelope she unfolded the fragile paper, "Look here Miss Kitty, this first one is from her son, Caleb. He has such strong manly handwriting; it will be easy to read. Let's see, he would be my great or perhaps my great-great Uncle. I'll ask Grams tomorrow which it is."

CHAPTER TWO

The First Letter - Caleb

Dear Paw & Maw,

Your letter arrived today and it sounds like your move to Oregon was the right choice for you. I've been praying the change in climate would help heal your lungs Maw.

It's almost Christmas already and the whole country is covered in a layer of white. Remember how all of us loved the first snow? Does it snow there? As always, I've been invited to the Well's family home for Christmas, so I'm going with Sam, Mattie and their kids. Evin will be coming and if Matt is around I'm sure he'll show up too.

This probably won't come as much of a surprise to you Maw, but I've asked Mary Louise to marry me and she's accepted. I pray you might be well enough to come for our

wedding. She will write and let you know all about the plans that are being made.

I miss you. Give all the kids a hug for me.

Love, your son Caleb

The wind was howling just as it had been for days and the snow was beginning to pile up against the cabin. It was snug inside however, with the fireplace giving off its warm heat and a lamp offering a soft glow to the room. Caleb was sitting at the table writing to his paw and maw. They had left that summer for Oregon where his paw's family had settled years before. When the doctor informed them that his maw had to have a warmer climate or her lungs would never heal, they knew it was time to leave. His two sisters and younger brother had gone with them while he stayed behind taking possession of the homestead they had settled on in Willow Creek.

Sitting alone at the table this evening he had to admit to himself, he felt a bit lonely for all of them. Suddenly there was a loud knocking at the door.

"Hey fellow, you home?" A voice called out.

Caleb rose to open the door and Matt Groves came in covered with snow. Matt was the youngest of the Groves brother's. These boys had been his paw's best friends and had helped him get established upon his arrival in Willow Creek, so many years ago.

"What in the world are you doing out in this weather Uncle Matt?" The Groves brothers had always been called uncle by all of Joseph and Margaret's children.

"Ah, it ain't all that bad. Besides, I thought having supper with another old bachelor was better than sittin` alone in my cabin or at The Palace."

"You know you're welcome anytime, it's good to have company. You haven't been around much these days. Been working a lot?"

"Yep, taking a few nights off. It's great having a job where I can pretty much work the hours I want. Besides, it's pretty slow, being so close to Christmas and all."

Gesturing toward the kitchen stove Caleb said, "I just put on a fresh pot, help yourself."

The two sat for a time in companionable silence, smoking their pipes and sipping coffee. They enjoyed the warmth of the fire as the storm outside seemed to pick up intensity.

Breaking the silence Matt asked, "So, have you set a date for when you and Mary Louise are gettin` hitched?"

The Wells family, the Groves brothers, and the Reeding families had all been neighbors and best friends for decades. Caleb Reeding and Mary Louise Wells had been sweethearts all the years they had grown up together.

"We thought to wait until spring in hopes that Maw might be well enough to come to the wedding."

Leaning back comfortably in his chair, Matt began, "It's funny you know, how things change over the years in our families; Brother Sam and Mattie having all those kids, along with his being the owner and operator of the town's newspaper. Evin is the town mayor, married to Angela and now you're gettin` married to Sam and Mattie's oldest girl. Heck, this leaves me the only one not hitched, and not likely to be. Yes sir-ree it sure is funny how things work out."

"Well Matt, what about Vi, Mattie's sister? You two have been close for years, and we thought you two might be getting together."

"Aw, she's like a sister to me, not a gal friend. She always loved this land and living here. I always felt that urge to see the other side of the hill and like, spread my wings, you know what I mean? Besides she's been gone to that school in Boston studying. When she graduates who knows if she'll come back here.

"I believe you're just using that as an excuse old fellow, and not meaning to butt in, but aren't you getting a bit old to be wantin` to spread your wings?"

Matt laughed. "You might be right, but sometimes a fella` hast to do what he hast to do. Like you pointed out, I ain't gettin` any younger."

"Is working at The Palace what you want to do from now on?"

"It pays good money and I like dealing cards. The place is real high class, the girl's don't go upstairs and, the entertainers are professional. The card games are honest, and heck he doesn't even water down the booze! I have a little place of my own, so I guess that is what I'll be doing for now."

"Well, not wanting to sound judgmental Matt, it's just that it's hard to think of you working there for the rest of your life. You know we all care about you and only want what's best for you. By any chance have you spoken to Father O'Malley about what you're doing?"

"Come on Caleb, you know what he'll say, about the same as my brothers."

"I'm not so sure Matt; you could at least give him a chance. You know he's pretty open-minded.

Matt interjected, "Sam, you do realize that I'm not just an employee, don't you? Blackie has made me a partner."

"Oh, I didn't know that! Congratulations!"

"Say, how about some stew?"

"Man, I thought you'd never ask! I'm starved!"

CHAPTER THREE

The storm had let up and everyone was able to attend church Christmas morning. The gathering at Hector and Maude Well's home was underway. Mary Louise, the eldest of the Wells children, and Caleb were still receiving congratulations on their engagement.

The Well's home had seen many a gathering of friends and family over the years. There was a stability and warmth there that just made a person want to be a part of this wonderful family. The Groves brothers had been taken under Maude's motherly wing when they first arrived. Hector had been like a surrogate father, helping them get established on their home stead. His age and wisdom were just what they needed, having come from an abusive background.

When Caleb's paw Joseph Reeding arrived in town, he had been welcomed by both the Wells Family and the Grove brothers. Later, when Joseph married Margaret, the three families had continued to grow in closeness as they faced the hardships and blessings of settling in the new town of Willow Creek.

That afternoon when dinner was announced, there was a mad scramble as the children began finding places at the long table. The women got the last minute items from the stove and put them on the table. There were piles of steaming green beans, corn, sweet potatoes, ham, rolls, butter, jam, along with a container of gravy, and large pitchers of milk. Next, there came the huge turkey on an enormous platter surrounded by mashed potatoes.

Oo's and Aha's were heard all around the table as everyone started passing the filled dishes and platters.

Hector stood up saying, "Let us give thanks for this incredible meal. Lord, we do come *to You today, wanting to say how grateful we are for everything You've given to us, our homes, our crops, our families, and friends. We are humbled to have such a bounty set before us today, and for all Your blessings, we truly thank You." And they all said,* "Amen!"

The rest of the evening was filled with laughter as favorite Christmas stories were shared and the children played with their new toys. There was a variety of desserts that came with more coffee for the adults and hot cocoa for the children. A quiet peace settled on everyone as the evening came to a close and good bye hugs were exchanged.

CHAPTER FOUR

Matt sauntered into Blackie's Palace and sat at his usual table. Looking around, he was once again filled with wonder at the lushness of this place. Gathering his deck of cards, he began to shuffle them. Sitting there was Grizzly McGraw, an old fellow who spent a good part of his days during the winter and early spring months right there in that chair.

There was no one else at his table but Matt fingered his cards anyway, mostly out of habit. He looked up when the old man began to speak to him.

"Where you been Matt? Missed you these past few days."

"Holidays are family days Grizz. I went to my brother Sam's home and stayed for a few nights. It sure is good to be back here though."

"Not a family man yourself?"

"Naw, a few days around all those kids is enough for me. I'm grateful to come back here and relax," Matt chuckled. "You have any family Grizz?"

The old man sighed, “When I was just a young squirt, I lived in the city and was married; after a few years we adopted a little girl. Then my wife, Molly, died of the influenza. The girl was only seven. I was tired of city living and wanted to head west after losing Molly. Rather than bring Pepper, her given name is Patricia, west with me, my sister suggested that I leave her with their family. Pepper, being so young, it seemed the right thing to do. But we’ve kept in touch over the years by golly.”

“You never mentioned a daughter Grizz, how come you never said nothin` about her before?”

“I don’t recon` I know. Just never came up I guess. I did talk about her a bit ago, guess you weren’t around.” Reaching into his pocket Grizz pulled out a piece of paper.

“See here, Pepper is coming to visit. She’ll be arriving by train tomorrow or the next day, let’s see,” he glanced at the paper in his hands.

"Why is she coming now? Has she ever been to see you before?" Matt was curious.

"Nope, but she writes pretty often. I told her she could come see me anytime she wanted. She just turned 18 and accordin` to her letter, appears she's wantin` to visit now. Ya` think she might have a bit of wanderlust, like her old paw?"

"Maybe so! Does she realize you live in an old cabin with no running water and an outhouse?"

"Yep, told her all about me and how I live and she wants to come anyway."

"Well I'll be! How long has it been since you've seen her? Are you sure you'll recognize her?"

"Oh shor`, she has red hair you can't miss. And she wrote that she'll be wearin` a brown dress and a green hat."

Grizz looked around The Palace and said, "This here place is so extra nice with its fancy carpeting and tile floors. Gosh, that horse picture over the bar would impress anyone who saw it. I think she'll love it too. I'm lookin` forward to showing her around.

You'll have supper with us sometime won't you Matt?"

"I'll look forward to it, Grizz."

Just then there was a ruckus across the room, near the bar. Voices got louder and it sounded like some punches were being thrown. There was loud cursing and gunshots were fired. Some of the girls screamed in fright, ducking down to avoid being part of the scuffle. Men knocked tables over in their haste to get out of the way. There were cards and chips flying everywhere.

Matt and Grizz hit the floor, scurrying behind an upturned table to avoid any stray bullets coming their way. Regretfully, one of them did.

CHAPTER FIVE

Matt turned his attention to the old man and saw he was gripping his shoulder. "You hurt Grizz?"

"I'm thinkin` it ain't the best day I've ever had son."

Matt yelled over his shoulder, "I need some help over here, a man's been shot. Send someone to town for the Doc."

Now The Palace was a good ways out of town, and it would take some time for the doc to arrive. Something had to be done to help the old man now. Fortunately, one of the hostesses had experience tending gunshot wounds and she quickly moved through the crowd making her way to Grizz's side. Bending down she opened his shirt to examine his shoulder and chest. Looking up she said, "Looks like the bullet went straight through, probably caused some damage but at least it's a clean wound."

Standing up, she asked a couple of the men to help move the old fellow to a room. Matt stood aside, and then followed them upstairs. When Grizz was settled, he sat with him until the Doc showed up.

Downstairs, The Palace was already back to normal. The piano played a lively tune and sound of clinking glasses and laughter filled the room. Tables had been righted and card playing resumed. The bar was doing a lively business and the girls were all smiles again now that the excitement had passed.

When Doc Hadley arrived, he was taken upstairs where Grizz was lying in a spare room. Doc examined the wounded shoulder.

"That gal who helped you did a good job of cleaning you up there old fellow. Oh, you'll be sore and stiff for a while, but if you keep the wound clean it should heal just fine. It's important that you stay down, don't put any strain on that limb."

"Thanks for comin` all this way Doc, have a drink on me." He looked over at Matt, "OK?"

"Come on Doc, I'll join you. Grizz needs to rest anyway."

Matt and the Doc stood at the bar enjoying a beer. "You don't get out this way much, do you Doc?"

"Sure don't, your boss runs a right clean place. I do have to come out for the homesteaders and the outlying ranches at times. But for the most part, these settlers are pretty self reliant folk. Every once in a while a wagon comes racing into town with an injured cowboy or work hand for me to fix up. But they don't come to me unless they absolutely have to."

As they were finishing their drinks, Matt looked up at the painting that hung over the bar and commented, "I'm sure glad nothing happened to that painting. Blackie would be furious!"

Looking up at the picture Doc said "No getting around it, that horse is one magnificent animal. I understand Blackie owns it."

"Yep, he keeps it in Mexico."

"Well," Doc said, "It's a long way back into town, guess I'd better be getting on my way. Thanks for the drink Matt, see you." With a wave of his hand he climbed into his buggy. Giving his Grey the reins, he lowered his head for a snooze.

Sitting back at his table, one of the regulars sidled up to Matt, "Tough break the old man getting shot like that. Don't imagine the sheriff will be showing up, too far from town, and it was an accident, right?" He sounded a little worried.

Matt looked at him, "You ain't in any trouble are you?"

"Not so the law would notice," he replied.

Matt queried, "Just what went on over at the bar anyway?"

"Don't know for sure, some cowboy took exception to something another one said, words were exchanged and then blows were thrown, you know how drinkin` men can get out of hand."

"Yea` I've seen it a few times, but not here; Blackie will track down what happened and who was responsible. He's adamant about keeping this place out of trouble with the law. That cowboy must have had a well hidden gun. You know that all guns are forbidden inside this building.

Later that evening Matt went up to see how Grizz was getting along. He seemed to be sleeping but as Matt turned to leave the room he heard him call out. "Matt, come over here son, I need to ask you something."

Matt sat in the chair next to the bed and leaned down so he could hear the old man. His face looked pale and he grimaced in pain. Shifting on his side to face Matt he said, "Dat-rat it anyway, what a thing to happen now. Matt, I need for someone to go to the train and pick up my girl. Can you do that for me?

Matt was taken aback and hesitated some before answering, "Ah, sure Grizz, I guess I can do that."

"Remember, she wrote she'd be wearing a brown dress with a green hat. I told you she has red hair and green eyes, pretty little thing. I've already arranged with Sophie for a place at the rooming house for her. So you can take her straight there to get settled in."

As he was leaving the room Matt said, "Well then, that's one worry you don't have tonight. Get some rest, old fellow, and I'll see you tomorrow."

Matt retuned back downstairs where he sat at his table thinking about all that had happened that evening. Life sure can throw you for a loop in a hurry he thought.

CHAPTER SIX

The Second Letter - Mary Louise

Dearest Mother Margaret,

We can't tell you how much we hope that you and the family might be able to attend our wedding. It's still several months away, do you think there is any chance that's a possibility?

As I sit here on your front porch writing this letter, I look out over the yard and fields that were so familiar to you. You always made this house so comfortable and warm, making everyone feel so welcome. I pray that it will always be that way as this becomes my home. I think of the years I was growing up and coming over here to visit. Secretly I always hoped in my heart that one day I would be a part of your family. And now I'm to be Caleb's wife! My heart is filled with gratitude to you and Joseph for raising such a fine son.

Something interesting is going on with Uncle Matt. He has been asked by an old friend to pick up his young daughter, who is arriving on the train tomorrow. We'll be looking forward to meeting her; a new face in town is always exciting.

Love, Mary Louise and Caleb

Pepper, Grizzly McGraw's girl, was sitting in a rather uncomfortable club car on the train that she had been on for the past two days. She felt rumpled and tired. She had a tiny room with a small bunk-bed for which she was grateful. It certainly was much better than sitting up all night. A few minutes ago the conductor had assured her that they were only about two hours from Willow Creek. She smiled and thanked him for having been especially kind to her during the trip.

She wasn't what could be called a beautiful girl, but still she turned a few heads on the train. Her hair was long, shiny, and dark red. She had wide set green eyes, a small nose, and a full mouth. When she smiled her face lit up, but there hadn't been much smiling in the past few days. She sat holding her green hat and purse thinking about seeing her paw.

She was excited and a bit afraid at the same time. What if he doesn't like me? After all, it had been years since they had actually spoken face to face. She remembered him as a kind man with a soft fuzzy beard that tickled her when he picked her up. He had been faithful to regularly send money to Aunt Alice for her keep. She liked his letters and always looked forward to them. Maybe she was being silly. Of course they would like each other! She felt sure of that. She could hardly wait to see him.

There were a couple of men on the train that insisted on paying her more attention than she wanted. She heard them talking and knew one was called Slim, although he was a bit chunky. She smiled to herself as she thought this. Then there was Dave, him she didn't like. He looked slimy to her, too slick, too sure of himself, a gambler she would have bet.

"I tell you, she's the old man's daughter! I heard his talkin` about her coming to see him just the other night when I was playing cards at The Palace." Dave insisted.

Slim answered in a hushed whisper. "If we grab her, he'll have to tell us where his gold mine is."

"You're thinkin` of doing that?" Dave asked, suddenly having a new interest in the girl.

"At the next stop we have the buckboard waiting with Limpy and Horace. Won't be no trouble adding her to our baggage is there? We'll get to our hideout and then send word back telling the old man we have his girl and to meet us to negotiate."

When the train pulled into the water stop, seeing that no one else was in the car, Slim walked up to Pepper and put his strong arms around her. She was shocked and had no time to yell when his hand went over her mouth. She was quickly pulled out the side door of the train car. She kicked and thrashed around trying to free herself. The stop was a remote one and the only sign of inhabitance was the buckboard parked by the water tank.

Limpy was surprised to see Slim carrying a squirming girl towards the buckboard.

"What you got there boss?" he asked.

"What's it look like dummy?"

"Horace, give me a hand. Get some rope and a blanket to put around her. Don't want any one lookin` out a window and seeing her. Once they had Pepper bound and in the back of the buckboard, Limpy stood looking at her, "What's this all about boss?"

"Opportunity came along and I took it," was the reply. "This little missy is going to get us that gold mine we've been talkin` about. Her paw is that old prospector Dave has been watching. I'll wager the old man thinks the world of her and I'll just bet he'll be glad to get her back in trade for the location of his mine."

"Come on. Let's get to movin`. The train will be in Willow Creek soon and then the alarm will be sounded about this little gal being gone. We need to be as far from this place as possible."

CHAPTER SEVEN

Matt had checked in on Grizzly that morning. He seemed to be feeling a bit better and was found lying quietly in bed. He once again told Matt what Pepper looked like and reminded him he was to take her to the rooming house.

"Be sure to tell her that I'm fine and she can come see me as soon as she's settled in." He seemed excited and kept telling Matt how grateful he was that she was being picked up by someone he trusted.

Matt was up and heading for town just before dawn. He wanted to be at the station in plenty of time for the afternoon train. It had been a long ride into town and he hadn't wanted to be late. He left his horse at the livery, having rented a buckboard to pick up the girl. He wondered if he would recognize her, but then there most likely wasn't going to be a lot of eighteen year old girls with red hair getting off the train.

The train pulled in on time and Matt watched until everyone got off. There were only two couples, a single man with a boy and the conductor. No Pepper. Maybe she missed her train and will be on the next one, but that wasn't due for another full day. Matt walked up to the conductor who was talking rather excitedly to the station master.

"Excuse me." Matt said, "I'm looking for a young lady, eighteen years old, traveling alone. She has red hair and is wearin` a brown dress and green hat."

The conductor stopped talking and looked over at Matt. "So am I!" He then continued in an agitated voice. "That young lady just simply disappeared."

Matt interrupted, "What do you mean, disappeared?" A sick feeling was building up in the pit of his stomach. "How could that have happened?"

"All I can figure is that at the last watering stop, she got off with those two men who were in the club car with her. It's not likely though, because she wasn't friendly with them, but it's the only explanation. She most likely was taken against her will, I'd say, because her purse and suitcase are still on the train."

Matt spoke up, "I was here to pick her up, may I have her belongings? I'll see about reporting her to the sheriff." The conductor boarded the train and came out a few minutes later with a suitcase, purse, and hat. "I'm mighty sorry I wasn't in the car to help her. She was a nice girl; I hope you can find her."

Matt got Pepper's belongings and put them in the back of the buckboard. Then he headed over to the sheriff's office.

"Hi Matt," Jeff Standish the sheriff greeted him. "How are things going with you?"

"As a matter of fact, things aren't so good Jeff. You remember the old man, Grizzly, who hangs around The Palace? Well, his girl was to have arrived on the train this afternoon, and it seems she's been abducted."

"Good grief. Give me all the details Matt."

****

It was with a heavy heart that Matt entered the old man's room upon his return to The Palace. "You look tired fella.` Did

Pepper get settled in her room? Will she be over to see me soon?"

Matt slumped down on the chair next to the bed "Listen my friend; I have something to tell you. Pepper has most likely been abducted. She disappeared from the train at the last watering stop along with two men who were also traveling on the train. The conductor is sure that's what happened. I have her hat, purse and suitcase, which were left on the train."

Grizzly was quiet as he put his head in his hands. When he looked up, anger was written on his face. He burst out, "It's that damn gold mine! I'll bet they think by taking her they'll find out where the mine is. Is the sheriff gonna` help find her?"

"He's already talked with the train's conductor and he said he would get some men together and go after her."

Quizzically Matt looked at his friend. "Grizz," he began, "you said something about a mine. There hasn't been a gold strike in Kansas as far as I recollect. What gold mine are you talkin` about?" The old man was hesitant, trying to decide just how much to share. “Guess I need to fill you in son, but I need your solemn promise that not one word of what I’m gonna` tell you goes any further than this room, understand?”

Matt quickly assured him that any secret was safe with him.

“It’s like this Matt; when I was much younger, I used to be serious about prospecting. You’re right, no known strike was ever recorded, that’s because what I found was really a fluke and I decided to never tell a soul. After all, it wasn’t really a big strike anyway. One night, when I had been drinking too much, I made the mistake of showing a nugget I carried with me. That started a rumor and it’s persisted ever since. When asked about it now-a-days, I just laugh along with everyone else pretending I’m just a little crazy. I made up a story about the nugget being won in a card game.”

“So there is a mine? Is it nearby?”

“You know Russell Springs, way up in the corner of this state, at Monument Rocks? Well, there’s a creek where I found a couple small nuggets. I followed the creek back up into the mountain, like I said it was a fluke. I found enough gold to pay for my little girls keep and schooling. I didn't take any of my nuggets into town ever again after making that mistake once. I took them up to Abilene. There was so much going on up there that no one took notice of an old man taking a tiny bit of gold into the assessor's office. It never drew any attention."

"And you think that someone believed the rumors of you actually having a mine after all, and that's the reason they took your daughter?"

"It's the only thing that makes any sense."

"Grizz, who knew she was coming?"

"I'm sure I talked about it ever since I got her letter, but only locally. Never noticed any strangers hanging around that might have picked up on that information."

"It sounds to me like it was a matter of luck that they found her and they simply took advantage of the chance meeting. What do you think?"

"I think I need to get up out of this bed and help find my girl."

"Now take it easy Grizz. The sheriff and his posse will go out to the watering stop and pick up on the wagon tracks. You can't do nothin` except hurt yourself by reopening your wound."

Just then there was a knock on the door. Matt answered it and found Father O'Malley standing there.

"I hope I'm not intruding. I heard about your injury and missing daughter. I thought you might like to have me pray for the both of you."

"That's mighty nice of ya` Father, come on in and sit yourself down."

Sitting, Father O'Malley opened his Bible and read Psalm 23. Then bowing his head he prayed, *"Father, we come before You with heavy hearts. You know about this young lady, and what she and her paw are facing right now. We hold them both up to You for Your courage and strength. Watch over Pepper Lord. And touch this injury that Grizz has sustained. Amen.*

Matt and Grizz agreed."Thank you so much for coming." Father O'Malley shook their hands and made his exit. Closing the door behind him, Matt turned back to Grizz.

"That was nice of him to come by."

"Yep, sure was."

CHAPTER EIGHT

The Third Letter - Mary Louse

Dearest Mother Margaret,

We are all well and having a wonderful time making plans for our wedding. I'm getting so excited. Maw is making my dress and we are planning on having the ceremony in our living room. We'll have the dancing and eating outside under the trees of course.Your last letter said that you were feeling better all the time. Is there any chance you might be able to come for the wedding?

Uncle Matt was helping out an old friend by going to town to pick up his daughter at the train station. Well, the strangest thing has happened, she has just disappeared! The sheriff and everyone else believe *she has been kidnapped. Can you imagine such a thing being connected to our little town?*

Matt is talking about going to look for her. He's just waiting until the Sheriff has made some inquires. I'll write you when there is more news about this.

We all sure hope to see you soon Mother.

Love,
Caleb and Mary Louise

It was a perfect day for the wedding. The sky was a teal blue with soft white clouds floating just beneath the sun. There was a cool breeze and everything indicated it would be a warm spring day. New leaves were appearing on the trees and yellow daffodils and purple hyacinths were peeking out alongside the house and under the trees.

The fields were blanked with new color from the green grasses and flowers.

The living room was filled with ferns and wildflowers so that it almost looked as if it was outdoors.

Mary Louise stood in front of the mirror in her bedroom admiring her wedding dress and the flowers she had woven into her hair. Her mother remarked, "You're a farmer's daughter and soon to be a farmer's wife. We don't have much occasion to dress up, and my dear girl, you look simply stunning."

"Thank you Maw, I love the dress you made for me, no store bought dress could be lovelier." Her mom's cheeks were pink with pleasure.

The music started up downstairs and Paw knocked on the door. "Ready my girl?" Opening the door Mary Louise reached for her father. He gave her a tender kiss on the cheek, "You're marrying a mighty fine young man honey. Come here Maw; let's hold hands as we ask the Lord's blessing on this marriage. *"Dear Lord, we humbly come before You with joy in our hearts over this marriage that will take place today. We ask Your special blessings on these two young people, may they always put You first. Amen."*

Mary Louise took her father's arm and they descended the steps that led to the living room.

There hadn't been room for one more person in the living room so they were over flowing into the hallway. As the bride and her paw descended the stairs, they parted to let them pass.

Mary Louise and Joseph knelt at the lace covered alter, placing their hands together on the open Bible. She glanced through her veil to look at the most handsome man she had ever known. She could barely hold back the tears.

After a short prayer they stood facing each other. Father O'Malley began to read the words so precious; "Dearly beloved, we are gathered here in the sight of God and these witnesses to bring together..." she didn't hear another word until she realized she was being asked, "Mary Louise Groves, do you take Caleb Reeding to be your lawfully wedded husband, to have and to hold, in sickness and in health, for better or worse, forsaking all others, until death do you part?" Her heart was pounding and then the tears came. She was overwhelmed with happiness and joy."Yes, I do," she answered. And do you Caleb Reeding take Mary Louise Groves to be your lawfully wedded wife, to have and to hold, in sickness and in health, for better or worse, forsaking all others, until death do you part?"

"I do," he replied. The next thing she remembered was the kiss and walking back down the aisle. She was now married to the man she loved more than anyone else in the whole world. She just knew they'd be happy and in love until the end of time.

The ladies from the church had decorated the tables that had been set up out under the trees in the side yard. There were chains of wildflowers and ferns laying down the middle of the longer tables. Bouquets had been placed in the center of the smaller tables. The food was arranged around the flowers and the tables were filled with every delicacy imaginable.

Caleb and Mary Louise, hand in hand, greeted everyone who had come to help celebrate with them. Pam, who ran the café, had made the most beautiful cake Mary Louise had ever seen.

It was three tiers high and decorated with pink and light purple sugar flowers. Green ivy wound through all the tiers. It was absolutely breathtaking. It was certainly the talk of the afternoon.

"You have contributed towards making this wedding even more memorable. Thank you so much Pam." Mattie hugged her.

The bride and groom were the first ones on the dance floor that afternoon and almost the last to leave it. As the evening progressed, the cool yellow moon cast a soft shadow over the wedding party.

Caleb took her arm as they dashed from the house to the buggy awaiting them out front. They were tickled to see it decorated in ribbons and streamers, with some tin cans hanging from the very back. Friends and family emerged, laughing and throwing rice. Smiles lit up their faces as they pulled away waving.

Her folks had reserved a place at the rooming house for the newlyweds, so they didn't have too far to travel.

At 1:00am the young couple was awakened by loud banging on the bedroom door. "Here we go!" whispered Caleb as he crawled out of bed.

They were both fully clothed for they had been sure their friends would be giving them a shivaree. When they opened the door, someone in the crowd hollered, "No fair!" They saw that they hadn't completely surprised the couple. Everyone crowded into the room banging pots and pans, making as much noise as possible. The party didn't last all that long and it ended with the couple being serenaded.

When the final song was sung, the door closed and the newlyweds collapsed in exhilarated exhaustion.

"Well, that was a fun way for us to start our honeymoon," Caleb remarked. They laughed about it like a couple of kids until sleep overtook them.

CHAPTER NINE

The four men set out across the flat plains toward some low rolling hills. The buckboard hit and bounced over the terrain as the horses were pressed on faster than was really safe.

Dave rode up next to the wagon and yelled, "You better slow down or you'll turn that wagon over."

"If I slow down the law will be on us before we can reach cover,"was Limpy's curt reply.

"Cover what cover? This state is as flat as a pancake, a so called hill is not more than a pimple on your chin," was Dave's sarcastic retort.

Pepper lay in the back of the wagon wrapped in a thick blanket which helped buffet some of the bumps. It was a terrifying ride. She was badly frightened and wondered what they were planning on doing with her. She closed her eyes and silently prayed, *"Dear Lord, I'm so scared and I need to feel You're with me. Please keep me safe and let Paw come looking for me quickly."*

It seemed an eternity before the wagon stopped. One of the men lifted her out of the back.

"Sorry for the rough ride Miss, but we needed to make as much time as possible before anyone missed you. I hope you understand."

She was surprised that the hands that lifted her down and took off the blanket and rope were gentle. She was grateful for the kindness. She could see they had stopped at a watering hole.

Stretching and brushing her skirt she asks, "W-w-why did you take me?"

"Well you see it's like this," Limpy started to explain when Horace, tall, blond, skinny, and cranky, interrupted.

"She don't need to know nothin` dummy, just get her some water and keep your mouth shut!"

Slim had gotten off his horse and walked over to where the wagon was standing. "She isn't hurt is she? The old man will be madder `n a she bear protecting her cubs if we hurt her."

"Naw`, she's fine."

The men intended to stop only long enough to water the horses and fill their canteens.

"You need a few minutes to yourself?" Limpy asked Pepper. He motioned towards a clump of bushes. She gratefully accepted for she needed to walk and stretch as much as anything else.

When she returned to the wagon, Horace was about to retie her when Slim stopped him.

"No need for that, we're far enough into the desert that there is no place for her to go. Let her ride on the seat next to Limpy." Horace scowled but did as he was told.

Riding more slowly now that they felt there wasn't much danger of the law catching them, Dave edged up next to Slim, "Just what do you intend on doing Slim? I don't remember us ever talkin` about takin` a girl to try to get the old man's gold."

"Like I said before, it was a matter of events falling into place and the opportunity presented itself, so I decided to take it. Can you think of a better way to convince that old man to tell us where his gold mine is, than in trade for his daughter?"

CHAPTER TEN

Matt was sitting at his usual table at The Palace when the sheriff walked in and sat down across from him.

"Howdy Jeff," Matt greeted, "any luck on picking up the trail of the men who took the girl?"

"We followed the wagon tracks until the wind wiped them out. It appears they headed up north. All we can do is send word ahead and hope someone in a town sees them and lets me know."

Jeff grimaced at the memory of the old man's colorful words expressing how he felt about not being able to join them. He said to Matt, "As you might image, her paw's pretty upset. With that bullet through his shoulder, he needs to stay in bed to guard against infection, besides, he knows we're doing all anyone can do right now."

That night Matt couldn't seem to get the kidnapping out of his mind. Sitting there dealing cards seemed so pointless. Abilene was the most likely place for those men to have taken Pepper. He found himself wondering why they hadn't received word telling the old man what they wanted in exchange for the girl. Did it really have anything to do with the rumor of a gold mine?

Matt made up his mind that he needed to do more to help find Pepper. Grizzly was fretting so badly that his wound wasn't healing and he was depressed. He cared for the old man and it just didn't seem right what had happened. Surely he could help. He would help!

Later that evening when Blackie put in an appearance, Matt left his table and went over to the bar where his boss was standing.

"What's going on Matt? You look worried."

Matt, explained to Blackie that he felt the need to help in the search for the old man's girl.

"I'd like some time off. It might take a while, but I really want to do this. I'm free to go while the sheriff can't leave his duties and traipse all over the country for any length of time."

"Certainly, you take all the time you need, just be careful Matt, and when you get back this place will be waiting for you. Good luck."

"Thanks Boss."

The next day Matt packed his saddle bags and headed back to town. He needed to let his brothers know what he intended to do.

CHAPTER ELEVEN

Heading north toward Abilene the buckboard gave a bumpy ride; Pepper almost wished she was still in the back wrapped in the blanket.

The men rode ahead so as to not get the buckboard's dust in their faces. Horace rode up beside Slim and asked, "Tell me again why we're saddled with that little girl."

Dave, who was riding on the other side of Slim, leaned over and answered, "Because her old man has a gold mine and we're gonna` use her to make him tell us where it's at, that's why!"

Irritated Horace shot back, "Who said her old man had a gold mine anyway? Did you talk to the girl? What did she have to say?"

"No, we haven't talked to the girl!! Tell me when could we have stopped to talk about anything?"

"Well, now is as good a time as any!" Riding back Horace rode next to Limpy and told him to pull up.

"Sure, what's up?"

The men got down from their horses and stood beside the buckboard. Horace directed a surly command to Pepper, "Get down and stretch your legs girly."

Pepper did as she was told, grateful in spite of feeling faint and fearful. He sounded angry for some reason. Facing her, Horace demanded, "How about you tellin` us where your old man's gold mine is located."

Seeing the complete surprise on her face, he chided, "Come on now, we know he has a gold mine and we want you to tell us about it." Completely baffled, Pepper answered, "I have no idea what you're talking about, Paw never mentioned a gold mine to me, never."

Horace slowly turned to Slim, motioning him to step away from the buckboard. His face was contorted with rage, "And you took Dave's word about the gold mine, without checkin` it out?"

Slim was getting angry himself and retorted, "And just when did I have time to check anything out? Dave said he heard at the saloon that the old man had a mine."

“Good grief man, we got a girl and most likely the law is trailing us right now and for what, a spur of the moment decision you made just because Dave said! This is crazy, we’ve got to get rid of her and lose ourselves before the law finds us.”

Horace fairly spit out his words.

Exasperated Dave asked, “And just what is your suggestion?”

“Let’s get to our hideout, and then we’ll take her into Abilene and dump her.”

She knows what we look like, we can’t just dump her,” Limpy whined. “You’re not talkin` about killing her I hope. I don’t mind being mixed up in a lot of stuff, but not killing anyone, especially not a girl.”

Slim growled, “Of course we’re not talkin` about killin` her stupid, just puttin` her someplace until we can get away.”

“And just where might that be?” Horace sneered.

“I don’t know yet!”

“What, no instant decision, spur of the moment answers?” Sarcasm fairly dripped from his words.

With that, Slim punched Horace full in the face, knocking him down. “If you don’t like how I’m running this outfit, you can leave; otherwise keep your mouth shut!”

Horace got up, rubbing his chin. He started to say something but thought the better of it.

While all this yelling was going on, Pepper was getting more and more frightened. She didn’t know what to do; what could she do? Out in the middle of nowhere, she was alone and there were four of them. *“Lord, oh Lord, help, please help”* she prayed.

“Come on, let’s head to the hideout and then decide what to do.”

Pepper had just put her foot on the wheel to pull herself onto the seat when the horses bolted, throwing her off the buckboard. She flew back, landing hard, hitting her head on a rock.”

“Stop that buggy!” Horace yelled as he and Slim jumped on their horses and raced after the buckboard. Dave and Limpy rushed to where Pepper lay, only to find her unconscious and bleeding from the back of her head.

"Just what we needed!" Dave said angrily.

"She's hurt and we ain't got no one to tend to her." Limpy was almost crying.

"Oh quit your blubbering and rip me a rag off the bottom of her skirt." Dave took the cloth Limpy handed him and bound her wound as best he could.

Slim and Horace came back with the horses in tow.

"The buckboard tipped over or we never would have caught up to it," Dave said. Seeing Pepper lying on the ground he demanded, "What's going on with the girl anyway?"

"She was thrown off the rig when the horses bolted and hit her head. She's still unconscious. I've bandaged the cut but I think she really could use a doctor," was Dave's reply.

"This is great, just great!" Slim was sputtering he was so angry. "What in tarnation spooked them horses anyway? We better hightail it out of here and fast, could be Injians."

They wrapped Pepper in the blanket once again and gently placed her in the back of the buckboard.

They continued heading towards the abandoned stagecoach station a few miles northwest of Abilene they used as their hideout. Riding carefully so as not to damage her wound further, they kept a sharp lookout for danger.

CHAPTER TWELVE

The Fourth Letter - Mary Louise

Dearest Mother Margaret,

You truly are my mother now you know. I am so happy I can hardly stand it. The wedding was just lovely. We really did miss all of you but we understand that you must continue to take care of yourself and travel just isn't possible yet.

Time has a way of getting away from me and I'm sorry, I've been so long in answering your last letter. We do thank you for the gifts you sent. I especially will treasure the vase. I have it in the middle of our table and put fresh flowers in it every day. You are so thoughtful.

Everyone is fine, the weather is holding and we have most of our fields ready for planting.

Uncle Matt came by the house sometime ago, heading for Abilene. Remember I told you he was going to help that old friend? Well, it turned out that the girl WAS kidnapped! My brother Gene went with him. Did you remember that we had my brother staying with us? We feel that Matt will see he is kept out of harm's way.

Caleb and I send our love ,
Mary Louise

When Matt arrived at Sam and Mattie's place he found his brother plowing in one of the fields. He dismounted near the tree line and waited for him to finish.

"This is a surprise little brother." Sam greeted him. "Come on up to the house, I'm through for now anyway, Mattie and the kids will be glad to see you too."

As they approached the house, Mattie came out along with several of the children. School had just gotten out and they were getting ready to do the evening chores.

"Uncle Matt!" They all greeted him at once. "What are you doin` here? You're usually at your card table about now, aren't you? Everything alright? You didn't quit did you?" The questions came tumbling from the children's mouths.

Mattie interrupted them by asking, "You stayin` the night?"

"Sure, if it's no trouble."

"You know you're always welcome, anytime."

Matt turned to the children and said, "Whoa there youngins! I'm just takin` a few days off, I'll tell you all about why I'm here over supper."

As Matt was washing up, Gene, Mattie's brother came into the room. "Hi Uncle Matt, good to see you."

Gene had come to live with Sam and Mattie earlier that year. He had just finished school and Sam relished having some extra help around the farm. Gene was a good looking kid, six feet tall, medium build with reddish hair and brown eyes.

Gathering around the table, Sam said the blessing, *"Lord we are grateful for the bounty You have provided for us once again. Bless our guest and this home. Amen."*

Matt was bombarded with questions again. He had just begun his story when their brother Evin and Angela came through the door. They usually tried to visit at least once a week for dinner and tonight was the night they made it.

"Matt! What a nice surprise. Don't see near enough of you these days." Evin chided.

Mattie took their coats and they sat down at the table. Everyone moved over a little and two more plates were put on the table.

Small talk was shared while everyone ate. When they finished, the younger children were excused and Matt then told about the events of the past few days and that he was going to Abilene to look for his friend's daughter.

Gene asked excitedly, “How about letting me come along with you? It’s safer to travel in pairs. I’ve finished school so I’m free, that is unless Sam can’t do without me.” He looked expectedly at his brother-in-law.

Sam looked at Mattie. “What do you think? Can we spare him for a short time? Matt could use another man along in case of any trouble.”

Mattie knew how badly Gene wanted to do something special after graduating. “I don’t see any reason why not. What are your plans after you reach Abilene, Matt?”

“Sheriff Jeff has contacted the Abilene sheriff, asking them to be on the lookout for two fellows and a girl. So I’ll go directly to the sheriff's office and see if they have seen or heard anything.”

Listening with interest, Sam interjected; “How about my running a story in the paper tomorrow? The train will be delivering the paper up the line and who knows, someone might have spotted them.”

“That’s a great idea brother, thanks a lot.”

The next morning, Matt and Gene were packed and ready to go. The sky was threatening, so just in case they had their rain gear out. Nothing could dampen Gene's spirits; he was so excited at the prospect of riding with his Uncle Matt to Abilene. It seemed to him that he had been in school and then working on the farm all of his life. Now at last he was doing something more exciting.

The two rode hard hoping to beat the rain before having to stop for the night. They were wet and cold when they came to a small ranch about forty miles out from Willow Creek.

Riding into the yard, they slowly approached the house. "Hello, anyone home?" they hollered. An old hound dog scrambled out from under the sturdy porch and began barking.

"Who goes there?" came a reply from inside the house.

"Riders, from Willow Creek, heading to Abilene."

"How many are you?"

"There are two of us. We just need a place to bed down for the night. Can we use your barn?"

"Don't see why not. You'll find grain in the back stall for your horses."

"Much obliged." They turned their tired and wet horses towards the barn. It was a large building, dry and welcoming. As they attended their horses they heard a voice coming from the barn door. They saw a figure shrouded in shadow holding a rifle on them.

"Turn around; I want to get a good look at the two of' ya'. Sonny, get that other lamp off that post over yonder and light it."

"Yes Sir!" Gene moved quickly over to the post and lifted the lantern off the nail. Reaching into his pocket for a match, he stuck it on his leg and put it to the wick. He turned the wick up and that corner of the barn was flooded with light.

"That'll do nicely.You wearin` a gun?"

"No sir, we only have rifles and they're on our saddles."

"Okay then," the rifle was lowered. "When you're finished with your horses, come on in the house. I'll have something hot for you to eat."

"We're grateful sir." Both Matt and Gene said in unison.

CHAPTER THIRTEEN

Having finished taking care of the horses the boys walked back to the cabin. Stepping into the small porch area they hung up their rain gear on the pegs provided.

When they entered the living room they were surprised to find that their host was not a man but an older woman. The place was neat and clean filled with the aroma of homemade bread. There was a long table, which surely seated at least eight or ten, running the length of the kitchen.

“Welcome fellows, my name is Henrietta Stiles.”

Extending his hand Matt introduced himself and Gene.

“I’ll bet you two could use something to eat. Sit and let’s see what’s on the stove.”

She came over to the table carrying a pot of beans and a large loaf of bread. She set them down and walked over to a cupboard getting down some bowls and spoons.

“Help yourselves,” she said with a smile, setting the items on the table.

“Sorry I called you a Sir,” Gene said as he greedily took a thick slice of bread and dunked it into the bowl of beans that he had ladled for himself.

“Don’t think anything of it; living out here, it don’t hurt for a minute to have a stranger believe their talkin` to a man. `Sides that, I have the All Mighty lookin` out for me, an` this here old dog.” She chuckled as she rubbed the dog’s ears.

“I’ll bet no man ever baked bread or made beans taste as good as these.” Gene said as he shoved yet another piece of bread into his mouth.

Henrietta asked what had brought them out on such a nasty night.

Matt replied, “We’re on the trail of two men and a girl. Any chance you might have seen anyone like that lately?”

“Seems to me I recall seeing four men and a buckboard a few days back, but I don’t believe I saw any girl with them. They didn’t stop, seemed like they was in a hurry.”

Matt turned to Gene, “Doesn’t sound like they’re who we’re lookin` for, but you never can tell.”

Matt filled her in on the kidnapping of Pepper and how they came to be following these men.

"That old man is mighty lucky havin` you two for friends. Sounds like you've chewed off a might bit for yourselves."

Changing the subject, Matt commented, "I didn't notice anyone else around when we rode up."

"The men are out rounding up the cattle before the really bad weather hits us. I have a nephew who lives with me, and five other hands. I know this place doesn't look like much when you pass by but I have a lot of really good pasture out back, and then too I can use some of the government's land for grazing."

"Even with help, living out here must be hard, especially on a woman I should think." Matt was remembering some of the hard winters he and his brothers had been through.

"You mustn't worry son, I've lived in much worse places than this. When I was married to my husband Harold, we tried to start a place up near the Canadian border.

That was cold like I've never felt down here." She seemed to shiver just thinking about it.

"How long you been on this place, if you don't mind my asking?"

"Let's see some twenty years now I seem to recall. When our place up north didn't allow for a decent living we drifted south and finally settled here. My Harold worked hard and he did good for us. A few years back he got gored by a rogue bull. Our nephew Ned, who was visiting, found him out in the hills, dead. After that, Ned just stayed on permanently."

"I'm really sorry for your loss," Gene said, "but it does seem you've gotten on well. Do you have any children?"

"We were never blessed that way, it would have been nice if we had but then you make do and are thankful to the Lord for what you do have."

"I didn't mean to pry," Gene said a little embarrassed.

"Oh my gosh, that's just fine. I'm made of good sturdy stock my dear," she smiled at Gene. "Well, you must be tired, get the lantern from the porch and you can make your way outback. Feel free to put a match to the stove, just rekindle it in the morning so when the men return it'll be ready for them."

When they had finished visiting she told them, "Turn right around the corner of the house, you'll see the bunk house down past the privy."

After settling in the bunk house and warming it up, Gene sat on the edge of his bunk saying, "Weren't we lucky to have stopped here, Uncle Matt? She's really nice. I guess there must be lots of women who end up having to run a place by themselves if they lose their husbands."

"It's the way when a new frontier is being settled Gene, hard times are expected and you rely on good neighbors when those hard times come."

Gene and Matt had a good night's sleep and in the morning they were fed an enormous breakfast. The table was laden with ham, fried potatoes, eggs, cheese, buckwheat pancakes, biscuits, jelly, and a pot of coffee. Matt thanked their hostess over and over again. This woman really knew how to get a fellow off to a good start.

The rain had let up. Although the sky was still dark there was a ring of sun shining out from around the edges of the dark clouds.

Looking up to that sky Henrietta remarked, “Looks like you fellers can make some good time today, it’s gonna` be clear. You be careful now. If you’re back this way, stop. I’d enjoy seein` you again.”

“Are you sure we can’t pay for our keep and this lunch you’ve made for us?”

“Lordy, what would this land be like if we didn’t help out when we had the chance? You don’t owe me a thing, off with yah` now!”

Waving good-bye the men headed towards Abilene keeping an eye on the sky. They rode hard that day stopping only long enough to give the horses a breather and to eat the lunch that had been provided by Henrietta.

While resting and enjoying the delicious meat sandwiches, Gene commented to Matt, “I bet there are lots of widowed ladies out here. This land is sure hard on folks."

Matt agreed with him. "Not just widows ladies Gene, lots of widowed men too."

As evening descended they could see the reflecting lights from the town of Abilene. They were still about ten miles from town. Off to the north they could see what appeared to be an old stage coach stop.

"Should we head for town or make a detour and stay at that place?" Gene pointed to the old abandoned building.

"It would be cheaper to go over there, that's for sure. However we're both cold and tired and it's already dark. I don't think we want to try to find firewood or sleep on a bare bunk. How about we just head for town?" Matt suggested.

Little did they know just how close they came to finding Pepper, and trouble that evening.

CHAPTER FOURTEEN

When the gang and Pepper finally reached their hideout it was already beginning to rain. Inside it was cold and damp. There were some logs and a few pieces of brush lying beside the open fireplace. "Be careful not to make too much smoke," Slim cautioned, "we don't want to arouse anyone's suspicions about this place not being empty."

They brought Pepper in and laid her on one of the bunks.

"Is she conscious yet?" Dave asks.

"Nope, but the bleeding seems to have stopped. What are we going to do about her now?"

Just then Pepper began to stir. She opened her eyes and raised her hand to her head.

"Where am I? My head hurts." Limpy leaned over her, gently helping her to sit up.

"You had a bad fall girly, you really had us worried."

Attempting to sit up, Pepper felt dizzy. She held onto Limpy's arm to steady herself.

"May I have some water, please?"

He got up and went over to the bucket holding the fresh water they had gotten from the stream out back. He ladled some into a tin cup and took it over to Pepper.

"Thank you." Shifting her gaze to him she asked, "Who are you?"

"My name is Limpy, and what is your name?"

Thinking for a moment she said, "I don't seem to remember, do you know it?"

About that time, Slim and Horace came back into the room carryin` saddle bags and more wood for the fire. They had taken the horses into the old barn, rubbed them down and fed them.

Limpy turned in surprise, "She don't remember her name."

"Well now that's a stroke of luck I'd say," Horace muttered under his breath.

Slim went over and knelt next to the bunk. He looked at the bandage around Pepper's head. He started to remove it when she wrenched back.

"Ouch, that hurts!"

"Guess it's because of the dried blood, sorry, didn't mean to hurt you. That bandage needs to be changed. We used some material from the bottom of your skirt; it was all we had at the time you fell."

"I fell? What was I doing that made me fall?"

"You were riding with us in the buckboard when the horses spooked, you fell, hitting your head on a rock."

"I don't remember. Who are all of you? Do I know you?"

Each of the men looked at the other, wondering just what to tell her. Finally Limpy spoke up, "Naw, we're just friends of your paw's. He asked us to bring you to Abilene where he would meet you."

This sounded a bit strange to Pepper, but right now she was too tired and her head hurt too much to ask any more questions. Slim got a clean cloth from the meager store of supplies and rewrapped her head; she laid back down and immediately fell asleep. Limpy put an extra blanket over her.

"That was quick thinkin` there dummy, what are you gonna` tell her when she wakes up and wants us to take her to her paw?" Horace growled.

Slim spoke up. "Actually that was quick thinkin` Limpy. As soon as she can travel, we'll take her into town, get her a room, and tell her to wait for her paw. Then we'll high-tail it back here."

"She knows about this place, we'll have to move on," Dave advised. "I was gettin` tired of this location anyways. Town is spreading closer and closer to us all the time. There are thousands of cattle and hundreds of cowboys on the trail and more comin` every week or so. Yes sir-ree it's time to be movin` on I'd say."

CHAPTER FIFTEEN

The Fifth Letter - Jenny

Dear Margaret,

My, but it seems like such a long time since we last talked. I miss meeting with you in the café. I still go once in a while and have tea with Lydia. By the way she always says to tell you hello.

I saw Mary Louise in town and she updated me on your health. I'm so grateful for answered prayers and to know that you are getting better all of the time. She said your move to Oregon was a good choice and all the kids have settled in.

Talked to Mattie the other day and she told me Matt and her brother Gene, went off hunting for a kidnapped girl. There was an article about it in the paper. My, how our little town has grown, we even have our own weekly newspaper now.

I was just reminiscing about how special it was for me that you were here with me to share my daughter Emma's wedding. She and her husband, Brad, just had their third little boy. Where has the time gone? Guess I'm getting old.

Brad still works as foreman out at Canfield's big ranch west of town. Just wish they were a little closer, I don't see enough of the grandkids. Of course twenty miles isn't all that far out in this country, but in the winter we never see them. Don't mean to be complaining.

This has been an interesting summer for Emma, having Brad gone a good deal of time on a wolf hunt. Levi and I managed to squeeze in a visit with them and Emma told me all about it.

Love you dear friend, Jenny

Brad and Emma lived in the main ranch house on the cattle spread owned by Josh Canfield. He was an old cowboy who had come up the Chisholm Trail from Texas years before. He had been really young when he joined his first drive, but he knew even then what he wanted and was ready to pay any price for it. He rode from 1867 to 1871 with any trail herd that needed drovers. He was a ramrod for Charles Goodnight's first cattle drive. When the big drives were pretty much over, he worked for any ranch that needed help. Years of hard work and savings saw his dream of a spread of his own become a reality.

When Brad and Emma moved on to the ranch they were never treated as mere help.

Canfield's wife had died at a young age, when small pox's swept the country. They hadn't had any children and he never remarried.

When they met again in Willow Creek Josh asked Brad to come work as his foreman. Josh asked Emma if she would take charge of running the main house. She was especially pleased to be asked. His house was big and well staffed; all she really had to do was see that everything ran smoothly.

The ranch house itself stood in a windbreak of trees surrounded by out buildings. There were stables and corrals, a bunkhouse, an icehouse, a woodshed, and a smoke house. Further out were the henhouse and a pigpen, plus one of the privies. Attached to the back of the house was a washroom and storage room.

The three of them worked and lived together; it was as if they had always been a family.

CHAPTER SIXTEEN

One late summer afternoon when Brad and Josh were riding out to one of the line camps, they came across a dead steer. Dismounting, Josh examined the animal. "Looks like the work of a coyote or wolf. Didn't realize we had enough of them in these parts to be worried about, guess I was wrong." Upon reaching the line camp, he inquired if they had seen any coyote or wolves lurking around.

"Actually Sir, we have noticed an increase in them lately. We took a shot at a big wolf last week, but missed. He was a beauty. We thought he looked like a huge dog and tried to track him but lost his trail at the timber line."

In the weeks that followed there were more dead cattle. Each time it appeared that a pack had fed on the steer, for the carcasses were picked clean.

Once again, up at the line camp, Canfield and Brad were told about sightings. It appeared to be a female and her litter that were feeding on the dead cattle.

"This has got to be stopped be-fore that litter of pups become full grown. They've had a taste of easy pickings with my steers. It will only get worse as winter makes food even harder for them to come by."

The last week in September, Canfield, Brad, and several of the hands from the ranch were prepared to hunt for the wolves den and destroy the litter. They hoped to get the male and female also.

It was said that the year before a big male shepherd-cross had been left behind when a farmer had been forced to leave his place. The son's dog may have gotten hurt or the call of a female had led him into the high country. In any case the dog was missing when it was time for them to leave.

The boy was heartbroken about losing his pet. The family delayed as long as possible, but finally they had to leave. No one knew for sure if this was the wolf/dog they were looking for, but it seemed to fit.

The dog could have returned later to find his family gone, or maybe he simply stayed in the woods. Whatever the case was, he needed to be stopped.

Just out of curiosity one of the men asked, "Does anyone know what the dog's name was?"

"I do," another man answered. "I was in town one day and heard the boy call the dog Bo."

The morning the hunters left the ranch, the air had a distinct chill to it. The men were armed and prepared to stay as long as necessary to find the canine raiders. As they headed out from the ranch the land lay sprawled out before them, lit by the morning sunlight. They stopped at a quiet watering hole. Graceful willows lined the banks. There they found prints alerting them that this was a place the pack came to drink.

As they rode through the meadow there were clumps of mountain laurel, yellow and pink roses and antelope brush scattered along the bank. In just a few weeks the Aspen leaves would be changing with the season. The air would become much cooler with the possibility of pending snow.

The riders headed first to the line camp where the male had last been seen. They followed tracks back and up into the timber that lay at the edge of the ranch. The trail grew harder as the trees became thinner and the soil became rockier. There were so many leaves and moss on the ground that they lost the tracks.

"Keep lookin` boys, scatter out, we're bound to find the trail."

Josh and a couple of men headed their horses further up the mountain. The others went to each side so that they spread into what amounted to a half circle. Finally, due to the terrain everyone finally dismounted. Continuing to look around on foot they reckoned that the den would most likely be found high up and well hidden. Remounting, they rode up to where the timber was even sparser. The rocks became bigger and more difficult to get around.

Evening was quickly descending and the air was getting colder by the minute. Josh rejoined the main group. "Looks like we need to head back down for the night. We'll pitch camp in the meadow."

The night proved to be very cold. Each man put his bedroll around the fire and managed to get a few hours of sleep.

In the morning the first one up rekindled fire. The coffee pot was boiling and the bacon and eggs were in a large frying pan. The aroma of the breakfast was all that was needed to rouse the others.

After eating the men mounted their horses. They searched east and west again with no luck.

The third morning as they were breaking camp, Josh, who had left the camp hours earlier, returned. Grabbing a cup of coffee he said "I've found their den. It's well hidden all right and empty. We'll need to get where we can watch for the returning pack." The hidden den was about two miles away from their camp and high up the mountain to the northwest. Canfield had been out traveling by moonlight when he came across the trail leading to the den. Not wanting to leave a scent or any indication that man had been near, he had gotten down and brushed the ground as he retraced his steps.

He told the men, "I'm pretty sure the pack will have returned to the den by the time we get back up the mountain. Our best bet is to quietly surround the den and watch."

Knowing it was best to wait until late afternoon before approaching the den, the riders settled down for the afternoon. Some sat talking, some played cards, and another had brought along a paperback.

As the afternoon shadows began to appear they mounted their horses. Slowly and quietly they followed Josh. It was a hard ride and they needed to be extra careful. The evening shadows hid fallen tree limbs and roots that the horses could stumble over. When they were close to the den they spread out. Each man found a place he could lie down, concealed by brush. The horses had been left a good distance away where they could graze and not be nervous with the scent of the wolves.

The plan was a good one for the pack had indeed returned.

Earlier that morning when the pack had returned to the den, the male felt something was amiss. He couldn't rest. He tried to get the female to exit the den with him, but she wouldn't leave the pups. He paced back and forth and finally left, alone in the late afternoon. He headed up the mountain, fearing he knew not what, but just knowing something wasn't right.

Canfield's men arrived not long after the male had left the den. As the evening shadows deepened, a breeze picked up. Lying in the dirt was uncomfortable and it seemed like forever before the female headed out of the den. She was dead before she knew what hit her. Then it was just a matter of getting the pups out. It was obvious that the male had left and was nowhere around. They knew the gunshots would have spooked him off.

"I'd say that was a good day's work boys, let's go home."

The dog watched the men and horses leaving his mountain. His feelings were all mixed up. He was confused that his family had been killed. He headed further up the mountain where he found an abandoned cave. There he curled up trying to get warm, ignoring his hunger.

The next day he returned to his old den longing to briefly recapture the happiness they had shared.

Finally he turned and ran down into the meadow where he would find food… and revenge.

CHAPTER SEVENTEEN

When they returned to the main ranch, each man headed back to his own place. Brad stood on the back porch of the house and called to Emma, "Hey honey, I'm home! I'm too dirty to come in, would you please bring me out a pan of warm water so I can wash up?"

"I'm so glad to have you home safely," she said as she got some hot water from the kettle and took it out to him. After washing his face and hands, he stepped into the porch just outside the kitchen and took off his dirty clothes.

Emma heated up more water for him to take a much needed bath. As he soaked in the tub he told Emma about the hunt, and how they had missed getting the male wolf.

Slipping on a clean shirt and pants, Brad sat in front of the fireplace as the youngest of his children climbed up on his lap.

When Josh returned to the house, the children clamored around him as well. "Uncle Josh, where have you been?"

Josh loved this time of the evening, when he felt he was really part of a family.

After dinner when all the children had been bedded down, Josh, Emma, and Brad once again talked about the wolf hunt.

Brad said, "We're wondering just how he'll act after having his family killed. He'll either leave the territory or he'll kill for revenge."

And kill for revenge he did.

The ranchers for miles around were victims of his raids. No matter how they watched, or what traps they set, he eluded them. The winter began with a heavy snow storm. While the killing eased up, they were still concerned.

"I'm at my wits end," Canfield said to the ranchers when they met. "We've tried everything we can think of, and still he kills our stock. Anyone come up with any new ideas?"

One of the ranchers spoke up, "I think we need to hire a professional hunter."

Another agreed with him, "As you said, we've tried everything we know to do."

Canfield headed into town that week to wire the Cattlemen's Association in Kansas City for a professional hunter to come and help them.

The telegraph operator composed the message and sent the wire. Looking up at Canfield he commented, "We ain't had wolf trouble in these parts for ages, wonder what drew them down from the timber line this time?"

Canfield answered, "We're pretty sure it's just one big wolf, or it might be that missing German Shepherd that was left behind when the Smith family moved away last year. But whoever he is, we haven't been able to stop him, so we're asking for help."

"That sure seems like a right smart thing to do Mr. Canfield."

"Desperate times call for extreme measures. We sure enough tried to take care of this problem ourselves."

CHAPTER EIGHTEEN

A week later Josh went to greet the man that the Cattlemen's Association had sent, they met at the trains water stop a few miles from his ranch.

"Howdy," the young fellow said, as he extended his hand, "They call me Samson."

"Mr. Samson, I'm Josh Canfield and the head of our association in these parts. You are aware of our situation?"

"I am, Mr. Canfield, and I believe I can help." They climbed up onto the buckboard, and headed for the ranch.

Upon arriving at the ranch, Josh showed Samson his room. Sampson set his duffle bag on the floor and returned to the kitchen.

There Josh offered him some coffee. "Supper should be ready in just about an hour; for now care to take a stroll around the ranch?"

"I'd like that. Your place looks to be well cared for. If we have time, I'd really enjoy a short ride."

"Of course, I'll ask Little Joe to saddle a couple horses for us."

Later that evening some of the concerned ranchers were gathered in the ranch's living room. They were interested in hearing about Sampson and his qualifications.

Sampson was much younger than they expected an experience hunter to be. He was probably no more than in his mid-twenties, tall, and lean with a mass of unruly black hair, and dark eyes. They liked his easy manner and the way he responded to all their questions.

"You've worked with wolves before?" One of the ranchers asked.

"I've worked with both wolves and dogs for years. They are so close in behavior it's uncanny. When a wolf is raised as a dog it will always be a part of him. When a dog is raised as a wolf the same is true, only it's easier to retrain a dog. They instinctually want to please a master. From what I've heard, this wolf you are having trouble with might have once been a family's pet dog. If this turns out to be true it will make it easier for me to figure out how he will act."

He stopped for a minute to take a sip of coffee before answering another question.

“How long you been workin` for the association?”

“I’ve been working with animals since I was twelve and earned my way into this job with the Cattlemen’s Association when I was seventeen. I have a good deal of experience, and success also, I might add.”

The meeting went on well into the evening with the ranchers each telling what they knew of the dog/wolf’s behavior and his kills. At the conclusion of the meeting, the gentlemen adjourned to the adjoining dining room where a late evening snack had been spread out for them.

After everyone had eaten and the talk had died down, Samson announced, “Gentlemen, I’ll be heading out in the morning. There is one thing more I haven’t mentioned; if possible I’m going to try to bring this animal back alive.”

The ranchers looked at each other in stunned silence.

****

The dog knew when the man entered the woods. He lay hidden in some deep brush and watched him set up camp. He instinctually knew the man had come to hunt him, but he felt no fear.

The smells that came from the man and his camp stirred a longing his heart, something he hadn't felt in a long time. Memories of a warm fire; running with a boy he loved; peace.

But now he had harmed the ranchers, he knew he could never go back.

Samson had been on the trail of the wolf/dog for over a week. He felt confident he had discovered where the animal regularly traveled. He had found the old den, but he was sure he never returned to it.

Winter was quickly settling in as Samson set up his camp. Being careful not to appear he was trailing him, he wanted the "dog," as he thought of him, to get used to seeing him and smelling his campfire. Each evening he sat by the fire and cooked up savory meat knowing the draw of the cooking smells would entice the dog. He hummed and sang so that his voice became a part of the forest. He was sure the dog had sat and watched him more than once that week.

It was a slow process, sitting and waiting. Samson followed this same routine over and over so it was no longer strange to the dog. He made a practice of talking out loud to the dog and he began to softly mutter the name ‘Bo’. The smell of the meat and stew cooking became very alluring to the animal as the cold set in and the snow began to fall again.

The anger the dog had felt when he first lost his family seemed to have lessened. Now he sat and watched, listening to the man’s voice and felt that longing in his heart again.

At the end of the third week Samson put some meat out on the ground a few yards from his camp site. He then slowly moved away to watch and see if the dog would come for it. Again the next day and the next, Samson putting out the meat softly calling, “Bo, here Bo, come”.

Finally the hunger drove the dog to run and snatch up the meat. He growled as he ate; staying close enough to see, smell the man and hear him calling. “Bo, here Bo, come”.

The next week he placed the food closer to the camp site. It only took two days more until the dog came within a few inches of the fire. Sampson sat very quietly calling to the dog, coaxing him. The dog hesitated before grabbing the meat, keeping his eyes on the man.

The snow continued to fall. The lure of the man’s friendly voice calling his name, the warm fire and savory meat slowly began to overcome his fear.

Samson was elated, he felt that it was now just a matter of time before he could bring the dog off the mountain and take him home; he knew the ranchers could never trust the animal. This would make it easier to convince them to allow him to keep the dog; for he knew, he was indeed “Bo”, just a dog.

CHAPTER NINETEEN

The Sixth Letter - Mary Louise

Dear Mother Margaret,

We haven't heard from Matt and Gene in weeks. I hope Gene will be content to stay and help on the farm when he gets back. This adventure should last him for a while. I do hope the two of them return soon however, it's getting late in the year to be out on the trail. I know I worry too much.

The weather has held, no storms yet, just some rain which we certainly needed. Mother, I haven't mentioned it before, but we are expecting a little one. Because of the miscarriage I had last time, I didn't want to get any hopes up until we were sure everything was going to be fine. Right now I'm feeling good and am having so much fun knitting little garments for my growing wee one. We haven't begun thinking about names yet.

Always look forward to your letters.

Love, Caleb and Me

Matt and Gene checked in with the local sheriff when they rode into Abilene, so far there had been no luck in finding Pepper or the men who took her. He hadn't received word from any other town round about either. "Don't know what else to tell you fellows, except we'll keep on the lookout."

"Look here at the article in the paper." Handing over the newspaper he added, "It came in on the train a day or so ago."

"It's Sam's paper. Let's see what it says." Gene took the paper and began to read.

MISSING GIRL

Pepper McGraw, 18, red hair, green eyes. She was heading for Willow Creek when last seen at the water tower, mile 78. Possibly kidnapped by two men, who were seen on the train. One being short & stout and one being tall, wearing all black. Anyone seeing the girl should contact the sheriff in Abilene.

Shaking his hand Matt said, “We appreciate your help sheriff.”

Turning to Gene, he said “Let’s check into the hotel at the end of town. I saw an eatin` place back there; after we grab a bite, we’ll talk about what to do next.”

The rain had let up but they were still damp and tired. As they approached the hotel the sign read, ROOM $2.00 BATH

$1.00. Gene asks, "Have you got enough money for a bath Uncle Matt? I feel like I'm carrin` a ton of dirt in my hair alone."

Matt chuckled, "Me too kid, let's get cleaned up, and order some grub."

Later, as they rested on their clean but shabby beds Gene asked, "What's our next move Uncle Matt?"

"Well, in the mornin` we'll scout the town. Perhaps they are here and the sheriff just ain't seen them. Of course you realize we're lookin` for people that we don't even know and maybe there are more men than the two we know about. It's like trying to find a lost calf in the bush."

The next day they began their search. They went into every saloon, store, café, and Chinese laundry to ask the same question, "Have you seen a girl about 18, tall, red hair, wearing a brown dress? There will be at least two men with her and she won't seem happy. She's been abducted."

They received the same answer from almost everyone, "Nope, but we'll keep an eye open for them. Sorry to hear about the girl."

In the following days when the hunting in town didn't bring any results they widened their search. They went as far north as Chapman then back down to Bennington, up to Rock City and finally back to Abilene.

Some ten miles south of Abilene they came across the abandoned stage coach station. Night was coming on and they were tired, so they decided to stop. There was an old corral and in the barn they found a small amount of fresh hay. They unsaddled their mounts, wiped them down, and finding an old bucket went to the rain barrel just outside the barn door and filled it for them.

"It seems rather odd to find fresh hay, guess this here stop has been used by others and not all that long ago," Matt observed. "Let's check out the main building."

When they entered the shack it was with some surprise that they found wood already piled by the fireplace and cold ashes. There were a couple of old blankets on two cots. Nothing was on any of the shelves, but they could tell the place had been used recently.

When Gene sat on one of the bunks, his hand touched a piece of cloth. He picked it up and found what appeared to be dried blood on it.

"Look here Uncle Matt, someone was hurt and used this piece of cloth, its brown and looks like it's from a dress."

Matt took the cloth and examined it. "Your right Gene, it does look to be from a dress, and the fact that it's brown would seem to me that it might have been on the gal we've been looking for. Her paw said she would be wearing a brown dress. Good heavens boy, she might have been right here when we rode by here a few days ago. We need to take this into the sheriff."

"Tonight?" Gene asked, for he was bone weary from all the riding they had already done that day.

"Can't see the rush, tomorrow should be just fine."

They got the fire going and made a pot of coffee. Getting their bed rolls from the barn they spread them out on the bunks and settled in for the night.

The next morning they rode into town and found the sheriff. Looking at the soiled cloth Matt showed him, they concurred that it most likely was from her dress. The fact that it had a few strands of long red hair stuck in the dried blood alarmed them.

"I'll ask around again," the sheriff said, "you never know what we might turn up. Did you ask the doctor if he treated a girl with any type of wound?"

"Frankly, I never thought about asking him," Matt replied.

"The Doc is out of town right now, seems he had a medical emergency out at one of the ranches. I'll contact him when he returns. No sense in you staying here any longer if you have farms to get back to. I can telegraph you if there is any news."

"You know, I think we'll stay a bit longer, just to see what the Doc has to say." They did stay a couple more days but it proved futile. When the Doc told them he hadn't treated any girl, they had to admit that it was hopeless.

"How in the world am I going to face Grizzly?" Matt was distressed and angry.

CHAPTER TWENTY

"You've done all there is to do Uncle Matt. You can't feel bad about something you can't help." It was with heavy hearts that the two headed back to Willow Creek.

Matt took them home on a different route than the one they came in on.

"Where we goin` Matt?" Gene asked.

"Want to check in on someone."

"Someone we know?"

"I don't believe you've met them.

There was talk around town about a family that had moved into a rundown soddy about twenty miles out this summer. The family had five kids and they were in a pretty sorry shape."

"So you went out to meet them?"

"I did."

"And...?"

"And what?"

"What did you find out?"

"I found out they settled on an unclaimed piece of land. The man, Jeff Cummings by name, seemed healthy enough; but he and the family looked plum worn out. There were some noticeable improvements made to the soddy, and they were trying to get a garden plot ready to seed.

A few days later several of us rode out to help them fix the roof and shore up the walls of the soddy. We took some wood as well as some food, staples like potatoes, flour, salt, sugar, and a side of beef.

"That's one of the things I love about this country Uncle Matt, the way we help each other out."

"Yes, me too. And since I haven't heard about them for a while, I thought we'd stop and check on em`."

As soon as they approached the Cummings' soddy, it was obvious things were going well with them.

Jeff was in the field and waved to them, stopping his mule he walked over to greet them.

"Well, Matt it's good to see you."

"Hi Jeff, got a mule I see."

"He's borrowed from one of the ranches. Everyone is so helpful."

"Jeff, this is my nephew Gene Wells."

Jeff came over and shook Gene's hand, "Right proud to meet you Gene. You've got a mighty fine uncle there. He and his friends really gave me and mine a helping hand when we needed it."

Turning to Matt he asked, "Get down and sit a spell?"

"Thanks for the offer Jeff, but we've been on the trail for a while and need to get on home. Since we were out this way, I wanted to check in and see how you were fairing. I'm glad to see things have worked out for you."

Just then Jeff's wife came to the door. "Matt! How good to see you. Set down and I'll fetch a cold drink for you."

Matt looked at Gene, "What do you think kid. We got a few minutes to sit and visit?"

Grinning, Gene said, "Guess we can stop long enough for that."

The boys dismounted and walked over to a bench that was placed in front of the soddy's front door.

Sue Ellen came out with two cups filled with cold water. She was followed by two little girls, both looking timidly around their maw's skirt.

Handing the boys the drinks, she said to the girls, "Do you remember Matt? He was one of the fellas who came and helped us a while back."

The girls giggled and scampered back inside.

"We don't get much company, so they're a bit shy."

Gene smiled, "My sister has a passel of kids, so I understand. You have some boys also, right?"

"The two oldest boys are helping a neighbor today. I don't know where the other might be right now, but he's around."

Sue Ellen excused herself and went back inside returning with a cup of water for her husband.

Finishing their drinks, Matt and Gene thanked them and said they really needed to get on their way.

"Come back anytime, company is always welcomed."

CHAPTER TWENTY ONE

Pepper sat on her bed in the Abilene Hotel. They had told her to stay in her room until someone came for her. Slim had brought her some clean clothes and made arrangements to have food delivered to her room. They figured if she would stay hidden for at least a couple days they could make a clean get-a-way.

Although she had been down the hall to take a bath, Pepper had indeed stayed out of sight for several days. It hadn't seemed strange to her at first, because she had no memory of who she was. And her head ached so much, she just wanted to rest. The men who had brought her there had given her some magazines to read but no newspapers. She slept a lot, not realizing she had a concussion. Now she was beginning to feel a little better and no one had come to see about her. She didn't think she needed to stay confined to her room any longer.

When she appeared at the front desk, the clerk was surprised.

"You're feeling better now Miss?" he asked. "Your uncles said you had an accident and needed to stay quiet for a spell, they also said your paw would be coming soon to pay your bill and take you home."

Pepper was shocked. "I'm so sorry, but I can't seem to remember who my paw is or who my uncles are. I barely remember being brought here."

Startled at this news, the clerk called to the manager. He was a portly man with thinning grey hair, large eyes behind glasses, and a warm smile. "What have we here little girl, no memory? You wouldn't be foolin` with us would you?"

"Fooling with you? I don't understand sir." She repeated what she had told the desk clerk.

"Sounds like we need to see if the sheriff knows anything about this," the manager said, not unkindly. Turning to the desk clerk he said, "Send someone to fetch the sheriff."

Pepper was alarmed, "I don't know what's going on. Am I in trouble?"

The manager patted her hand and said in a soften voice, “Don’t you worry none. Since you’re lost, we’re just trying to find out if anyone is looking for you.”

The sheriff rushed to the hotel and there he found Pepper sitting with the manager. “She has lost her memory, likely from the gash on the back of her head.” The manager related what Pepper had told him. The sheriff listened attentively.

“I believe we did have someone lookin` for you young lady. Your name is Pepper McGraw and your paw lives down in Willow Creek. You were taken off the train by a couple fellers who were probably planning to use you for ransom. Maybe because you got hurt they changed their minds.”

Seeing that Pepper was looking pale, the men decided to take her back to her room where she could lay down.

“I’ll be back later little lady, you just rest for now. Everything is going to be just fine.” The sheriff left the room and said to the hotel manager, “I’ll contact those boys who were lookin` for her. You just allow her to stay and keep taking care of her, I'm sure they will pay anything that is owed."

True to his word, the sheriff contacted the Willow Creek sheriff about the girl. Later that evening he returned to her room to see if she could help identify the men who took her.

"Evening Miss, how are you feeling?"

"I am feeling better sheriff. Did you contact my paw about finding me?"

"I contacted the town sheriff by wire. The sheriff will deliver the news to your paw. Do you feel up to answering some questions?"

"Like, can I tell you about the men I was with? I can do that." And she proceeded to tell him everything she could remember, including what each man looked like.

"This is a real big help. With this information we should be able to track these men down. There's a good chance they've been in trouble before. They didn't harm you did they?"

"They were actually very decent. One especially was very nice, a simple little man named Limpy. None of them harmed me in any way. I hope they aren't in too much trouble."

"That will depend on what I find out, but don't you worry about them. You just rest easy until your paw comes for you. Has a doctor looked at your head injury since you've been here?"

"I hadn't seen anyone until I came down stairs today."

"Well then, I believe it would be wise to have Doc examine you."

CHAPTER TWENTY TWO

The Seventh Letter - Mary Louise

Dear Mother Margaret,

Gene and Matt have finally returned. We were so glad they arrived before the first snow hit us. We could tell by the looks on their faces that they hadn't found the girl. Worse, they believed they found where she was being held. There was a piece of her dress with dried blood on it. They don't know if she is dead or alive. I've never seen Matt so down. Well, on to happier news. I had lunch with our sweet school teacher Lydia. She admitted that she and Doc Hadley were keeping company.

Those two have been best friends for ages, and they're not getting any younger. I know I'm a hopeless romantic.

I'm so glad to hear that you have settled in and have made some new friends. You mentioned that Joseph wasn't feeling well, any idea what may be wrong? Be sure to let us know what you find out.

I'm as big as a horse and Caleb is so funny, you'd think he'd never been around anyone who was having a baby. He's been a dear to me and I'm so grateful. He had a neighbor girl come in this past month to help me with the chores.

Love, Caleb and Mary Louise

Matt and Gene were dragging when they finally arrived at Sam and Mattie's place; tired, dirty, and discouraged, they were glad to be back home. One look at them and it was evident that the search had not gone well.

After they had cleaned up and had eaten, Matt relayed to them what they had discovered.

"This bloody cloth, that's all we have to show for our time spent hunting. We don't know if she's hurt or even alive. I don't know how I can face Grizzly." Matt was so heartsick and tired; he could hardly stay awake at the dinner table. "Please excuse me, but I need to lay down." He excused himself and left the room.

Gene was quiet. "It was hard lookin` and lookin` and finding nothing, but even harder when we found the bloody rag, and of all the places, one we passed by on our way into town."

Sam sat and listened to Gene talk, for it was obvious that he needed to let out some of his feelings.

"You should be proud of yourself Gene, you and Matt did a real fine thing for that old man. At a time like this, he needed to have someone who would at least offer to help."

"I know Sam; we were so sure we could help find her." He sat hunched over and looking exhausted.

"I know you're tired Gene, head on to bed and we'll talk more tomorrow."

CHAPTER TWENTY THREE

Having put off returning to The Palace for as long as he could, Matt forced himself to leave his brother's place two days later. His heart was sick at the thought of having to tell Grizzly about their failure to find his girl and about the bloody cloth.

When he finally entered The Palace that night he was surprised to see Grizz sitting at his usual place at the card table. He looks old and tired, thought Matt.

"How you holding up Grizz?"

Looking up he said to Matt, "Guess you weren't able to find her. Well, don't feel bad, I know you did your best. Everyone's done their best."

"I'm so sorry Grizz," Matt started to say but he was interrupted.

The old man said in a low voice, "The Lord gives and the Lord takes away, blessed be the name of the Lord. But the Lord will have to excuse me because I'm gonna catch the scum that took my Pepper and I'm going to kill them." With teeth clenched, he got up.

"Where you goin` Grizz?" Matt asked.

"I'm tired; think I'll head to bed. Again, thank you for all you did, I'll always be grateful." He walked towards the stairs.

The local sheriff had gotten the telegram from Abilene just a few hours before. Knowing that the missing girl had been found and was safe he decided that he had to get this good news to Matt and Grizz immediately. He saddled up and rode hard, feeling he had the most important news he might ever be privileged to deliver.

It was well past midnight when the sheriff walked into The Palace. The place was lit up, with music playing. There were still a good number of cowboys playing cards. He walked over to where Matt sat slumped at his table, looking unhappy.

He looked up in surprise, "What brings you out at this late hour sheriff?"

"Good news Matt! The girl has been found, alive and well."

"Found! Where, when, oh never mind, stay here while I get Grizz. He's up stairs sleeping."

"Yahoo, she been found!" Matt hollered as he knocked on the bedroom door, "Grizz wake up, Pepper has been found!"

The old man bound off the bed where he had thrown himself fully clothed a short time before. "My girl's been found?" He seemed a bit dazed. "Who told you? Are you sure?"

"Grizz, the sheriff came all the way out here tonight to tell you that she was found and is alright. Come on! Let him tell you what he knows, he's downstairs."

The Palace offered drinks on the house for everyone that night, even the sheriff indulged in a beer. The happiness was profound. Sorrow had been hanging over everyone, and it was incredible. Handshakes, back slapping, and toasts were exchanged for the old man.

CHAPTER TWENTY FOUR

The very next morning Grizz and Matt saddled up and headed for town; where they bordered the train to Abilene. The sky looked bluer than they remembered it being, the grass greener, the sun wasn't as hot, and in fact nothing was the same and never would be again. They were two happy men.

It was hard for Grizz and Matt to sit quietly in their seats. They tried playing cards, they had drinks and talked but the time seemed to stand still.

"Can't help it Matt, I'm so all fired anxious to see my girl I can't seem to settle down."

"I understand, Grizz, we'll get there in plenty of time, she won't be going anywhere without us."

Each of the two men sat looking out of the window as the landscape crawled by, each deep in their own thoughts.

Grizz thought back to a time when he had felt complete. It seemed like only yesterday.

****

Grizzly McGraw and his darlin` Molly O'Donald had just become husband and wife. He was 28 and had wondered if he would ever meet the girl for him. He remembered the evening he had been talked into going to the dance by a friend. There he saw this vision, with flowing red hair and incredible blue eyes across the room and he knew in his heart, right then, she was the one!

Grizz was a huge man standing over 6 feet 3 inches tall and weighing 238 pounds. He had a shock of auburn hair and sparkling green eyes. He was a sailor whose ship had just docked in harbor and he had already decided that he wasn't going to sign on again. Seeing that girl cemented the fact that he wanted to be on dry land with someone special.

Grizz had left his ship here because his only sister, a widow, lived in Clarksville. He planned on staying with her until he made further plans. He'd already taken a job as an apprentice with the town's blacksmith.

It was hard work and it suited him, he was strong and a quick learner.

He returned to his sister's home that evening and announced "Sis, I've just seen the girl I'm going to marry."

"That was fast, anyone I know?"

"Do you know a Molly O'Malley?"

"I don't know her well, but I know she works at a dress shop over in Veron Hill."

"She's not married I hope."

"Can't help you there little brother."

"How far to Veron Hill?"

"It's only two miles from here."

"Great! I can walk that distance easy."

Molly lived with her parents, a younger sister, and an older brother on Elm Street.

This evening after the Friday night dance, she found herself day-dreaming about the tall, very tall, sailor she had danced with.

"Mom I think, just maybe, I've met the man I'm going to marry."

She was surprised as her daughter had never expressed interest in any one boy before.

"Tell me about him dear, I'm all ears."

"His name is Grizzly McGraw and he's just home from a tour on a merchant ship. His sister lives down in Clarksville and he's staying with her. She's a widow.

"A sailor? How long will he be here?"

"Permanently!! He isn't signing on for another voyage. He's working with a blacksmith for now."

"How did you meet him?"

"Tonight, at the town dance."

"You certainly learned a lot in just one night."

"I know, we talked and danced and talked and danced, all evening. Oh Mom, he was just wonderful!"

It was a whirlwind courtship with them staying in Virginia. They were ecstatically happy and planned on starting a family as quickly as possible.

Grizz was deep in his memories as the train sped towards their destination.

CHAPTER TWENTY FIVE

Molly McGraw continued to work in the dress shop after she was and Grizz were married. She had become special friends with one of the girls she worked with. Ruth was single and had a darling little girl named Patricia. Grizz and Molly often had Ruth and Patricia spend weekends and holidays with them.

On this warm summer day in the park, Grizz and Patricia were playing ball on the grass. Molly and Ruth sat at a picnic table watching them.

"Ruth," Molly asked, "you never mention your family, don't you have any?"

Smiling, Ruth answered, "My maw DeeDee, died when I was twelve. My father was a gambler on a river boat that ran the Mississippi. It seems he got into some trouble and left the country. Maw and me had nothing. It was hard for her trying to make a living for us; she was sick a lot."

"Was there no one to help you two?"

"I knew I had a grandmother someplace. Maw said she didn't get along with her at all. Seems Grandma was against the marriage. Maw told me she would never ask her for help. There was a painful gulf between them."

"So, your maw got sick and died, leaving you, with who? How old were you, twelve?"

"That's right, and since there was no one to take me, I went into an orphanage. When I turned eighteen I left there and went to work, like you, as a seamstress."

"And from there, what? Am I prying? I don't mean to be, I'm just interested, and after all we are best friends."

"Actually it's nice having someone to talk to about that part of my life. When I met my sweet, quiet John it was easy to believe I was in love. Unfortunately, he was attacked one night and left on the streets near the waterfront to die; they never found who killed him. In the mean time I found out I was expecting a baby."

"Oh Ruth, how awful!"

"I'll admit it was hard, but I still had my job and a place to live. The owner of the shop where I worked was very nice. I was allowed to work right up to the day I had my baby. Afterward, I was allowed to bring her to work with me."

"Patricia was such a contented baby, everybody loved her. Everything was good for a while."

"What happened, why did you leave there?"

"The usual I guess, the owner's son began making advances. I knew I had to leave. Fortunately this job opened up and here I am."

Wow, what a story. I'm so glad that everything worked out and that we met. You and Patricia have filled a hole in our lives you know. Grizz and I want a child of our own, but so far it hasn't happened."

One day, several months after this conversation had taken place, Ruth came to Grizz and Molly and asked them if they would become guardians to little Patricia if anything ever happened to her.

"Why Ruth, we would be honored."

It wasn't but two weeks later that a runaway buggy hit and killed Ruth as she was on her way to the market. Fortunately, the little girl had not been with her. Because the guardianship papers that had already been made up, it was easy for Grizz and Molly to formally adopt little Patricia. She was such a quick little thing so alive and sharp and well, spicy. So it just seemed natural to begin calling her Pepper.

Grizz and Molly took to being parents as if this darling little girl had been born to them. Pepper was young enough that the loss of her mother didn't appear to be an issue with her.

One evening, a few days after Ruth's death, little Pepper asked, "Is my mommy coming to get me soon?"

Molly took her on her lap and told her, "Honey, your mommy has gone away."

"When will she be back?"

"Not for a long time."

"She didn't want me to go with her?"

"It was a trip she had to take alone. She loves you so much, but you are going to stay with Grizz and me from now on."

Pepper looked at her for a long time, "You're sure it's alright with Mommy if I stay with you?"

"I am sure my darling."

Grizz and Molly looked at each other and gave a sigh of relief. There would be enough time, when she was a little older, to answer all the questions that she will eventually ask.

****

Grizz was thinking how good life was as the train sped towards the town that would reunite Pepper back with him. His chest constricted a bit when he thought of how they had only had four years together with little Pepper before Molly died. He still felt they had been the best years of his life.

The silence was broken when Matt asked, "Hey Grizz, where you been, I've been talkin` to you for ten minutes and you haven't even heard me. You okay?"

"Ya, ya I'm fine, I was just remembering back when it was Molly and me and Pepper. We was a real happy family."

CHAPTER TWENTY SIX

The Eighth Letter - Mary Louise

Dearest Mother Margaret,

Well, Mother, we have a darling baby boy. Caleb wanted to name him Peter after your father and his grandfather.

You know, having been around babies all my life still never prepared me for the joy of having my very own. I'm sure you know just what I'm talking about.

More good news! The girl that was abducted turned up in a hotel in Abilene. She had lost her memory from a hit on the head but otherwise seems to have come through the ordeal all in one piece. Matt and her paw, Grizz, picked her up and returned as happy as I've ever seen any two men.

Matt and Gene had been so dejected when they came back without her. The Lord really is so good, how would we ever survive without His grace to see us through?

I believe Gene has had his fill of the big city for awhile. He will be staying with us for the winter and then decide what to do next. There has been a whistle on his lips ever since he received the news about the girl being found.

Love, Caleb, Mary Louise, and little Peter

The two men rode straight to the hotel when they got to Abilene. Dusting themselves off a bit, they headed right for the hotel desk. "We'd like to see the manager The two men rode straight to the hotel when they got to Abilene. Dusting, please," Grizz said to the clerk behind the desk.

"May I ask what it's about, sir?"

"Yep, it's about the girl you're takin` care of. I'm her paw."

"Oh gracious, yes sir, hold on sir, I'll get the manager."

The clerk scrambled over his own feet getting out from behind the desk and heading towards a polished door marked "Manager".

It only took a moment for him to come out of his office. He stuck out his hand, "I'm so glad to meet you sir, shall we go up to your daughter's room? I know she will be anxious to see you."

As they approached Pepper's room, Grizz began to have second thoughts about just popping in.

Turning to the hotel manager he said, "Wait! You knock on her door and let her know we are here." He turned and almost ran down the stairs.

Following him to the lobby, Matt asked, "What was that all about Grizz?"

"You said she had lost her memory, don't you think it would be better not to just barge into her room? She most likely won't remember me. I don't want her to be any more anxious than necessary."

It seemed like a lifetime to Grizz and Matt before a lovely young lady appeared at the foot of the stairs. The manager was standing beside her, holding her arm as if to steady her.

Stepping forward, Grizz said, "Hello there Pepper, do you know me?"

Pepper looked at this huge man and immediately liked him. "I'm sorry sir, but I don't recognize you. Did they tell you I had an accident and I haven't regained my memory yet?"

"Yes, they did. May we sit down and talk a little?"

Matt felt a bit out of place and quietly excused himself to go next door for a drink; Grizz nodded.

The manager led Pepper over to the divan under the big window and left them alone there to get reacquainted.

"Well, where do we start? How about I'll tell you about myself, it might help you remember."

For the next hour the two of them sat side by side talking. When it was time for supper, they ask Matt to join them in the dining room.

It was obvious Pepper was tired, and maybe just a bit overwhelmed, so Grizz walked her back to her room. "I'll be back in the morning. We'll have breakfast together. Then you can decide what you want to do next." With that, he left her and headed back to the lobby.

"Do you have a room for us?" he asked the manager.

"Certainly sir, you'll be staying how long?"

"I really don't know, but I'll settle up for the girl's keep before we leave."

"That will be fine. I'm so glad you found her. She seems like a very sweet young lady."

"She is sir, believe me, she is."

The next morning they all met in the dining room for breakfast. Grizz sat looking at Pepper, grateful they had found her.

She looked up at him and smiled. She had decided during the night that she would go home with this man who called himself her paw. She was weary and longed to put the past weeks behind her.

"I'd like to go home as soon as possible," she announced as they finished eating. Holding out her hand to Grizz, "Is that okay with you?" "Nothing in my whole life has ever been more okay." Grizz took her hand in his and pressed it to his cheek.

The three of them boarded the train back to Willow Creek that very afternoon. It would take some time to adjust, but they were optimistic thinking of the days ahead.

CHAPTER TWENTY SEVEN

Bonnie put down the letters and sat in her chair for long time thinking about what she had just read. Finally she got up, washed her face, brushed her teeth and put on her nightgown. Crawling into bed she fell asleep dreaming about the kidnapped girl, killer wolves, and a wedding all jumbled up together.

In the morning she slowly made her way down the stairs and into the kitchen.

"Good morning everyone."

"Well, good morning to you too sleepyhead." Her mom and grams were standing at the sink washing dishes. Her dad had already left for work and the younger siblings were all off to the park. Being summer, there were lots of activities for them, summer leagues, swimming classes, and of course picnics.

Grabbing a coffee and a sweet roll she said, "Well, guess I had better get myself down to the pool before they hire someone else to lifeguard!"

When Bonnie got home that afternoon she was tired, so taking a nap seemed like a good idea. As she drifted off to sleep she dreamed she was riding in a buckboard not knowing where she was going. Then she was sitting down with Jenny in the coffee shop hearing about Brad and the wolf hunt. She woke with a start. "My gosh!" she muttered, "I feel like I'm living back in Willow Creek." The next day Bonnie went with the family to her aunt and uncle's home in a nearby town. It was a good break for her. It was her cousin's birthday. Bonnie was anxious to stay behind for a week. She and her cousin had some fun things planned.

Bonnie returned home looking forward to resume reading her gram's letters. She unpacked and helped get dinner ready that evening. Mom asked, "Did you get to do some interesting things with your cousin?"

"We did a lot of swimming, took in a couple movies, and even attended a baby shower. All in all, it was a fun week.

Later, Bonnie headed up to her room where she took a bath and got into a comfy gown. She was then ready to settle down with the next stack of letters, and with Miss Kitty.

CHAPTER TWENTY EIGHT

The Ninth Letter - Jenny

Dear Margaret,

I was glad when your last letter came telling me that you were given a clean bill of health. We're saddened to learn that Joseph is still so ill. The doctors don't know for sure what is wrong? You know our prayers are with all of you.

It's wonderful news about your new grandson, Peter. He is the absolute picture of perfection! So cheerful and chubby! Mary Louise simply glows. Caleb is swelled up like a toad, he's so proud.

I still work with Doc Hadley upon occasion, but I'm getting pretty crippled up. My leg bothers me a lot these days. When it's really cold I spend a good deal of time beside the fire. I hear that the town will be getting another doctor soon, so that will mean I won't be so needed. I know I'll miss not working with Doc Hadley.

One evening when we were visiting, Brad told us more about his background. Over the years, snatches of his life were mentioned, but we never took the time to just sit down and listen to his story. I know it seems funny, guess it simply never came up. We all have stories don't we.

Love you dear friend, Jenny

Brad Kellerman and his folks lived in Arizona on a fair sized ranch that had been settled by their great-grandfather Bud Kellerman Sr. in the early 1800's. Brad had five brothers and two sisters. The two girls were married and had homes near the main house. Two of the brothers had been killed in the civil war. Two had chosen to stay on the ranch while Brad, the youngest boy, was looking to join a cattle drive.

Brad, was 6' 2" tall and weighed 185 pounds, looking much older than his fifteen years. He had broad shoulders muscular arms, and a strong back. He enjoyed working on the ranch, especially with the cattle and horses. He was a gentle young man, but determined once he set his mind to something.

A man named Charles Goodnight was forming up one of the very first cattle drives from Texas. He would be heading up to Fort Sumner, and Fort Bacon in Indian Territories,* (*later to be named New Mexico) because the army was badly in need of beef.

Every since seeing the article about the cattle drive, Brad had been thinking about the chance to join up with them. He longed to do something new, something different, an adventure!

Bud Kellerman Jr., Brad's paw, was a God fearing, hardworking family man whom Brad greatly admired. It was natural that one evening when Brad and his paw sat by the fire in their spacious living room, that Brad began discussing his desire to join the cattle drive.

"Well son, I can see that you're serious about the cattle drive that everyone' talkin` about. What makes you think you can find a place with that outfit?"

"Paw, you saw the piece in the paper. It says that anyone who thinks they can survive a thousand miles of bad weather, dry camps, Indians, and two thousand wild longhorns, were to report no later than July 21st at Horsehead Crossing on the Pecos River in Texas. Bring a good horse, rope, and gun; they would take care of the rest."

"Somehow that doesn't sound very inviting to me. They certainly don't paint a pretty picture of what this ride will offer you. Have you talked about this with anyone else?"

"Yep, in fact Jody Remstead and I have talked a lot about what it would be like. He wants to go with me, so you see I wouldn't be on the trail without a partner."

"Have Jody's folks given their approval?"

"They have Paw. We both really want to be in at the start of this new drive, to be part of heading up those wild longhorns. That's some of the adventure we're craving."

"Certainly sounds like an adventure alright, and you've given this trip your full consideration son? I'm a little concerned that you might not realize just what you'll be letting yourself in for."

"You might be right Paw, but I want to try. After all, someone hast to be part of breaking new trails and I believe it will be young men like myself and Jody who will do it. I'm fit, can shoot, rope, and ride. I'm hopin` you and Maw will give me your blessing."

His paw started to say something but Brad kept talking, "Grandpa Kellerman took a risk when he settled here with his paw. Arizona wasn't well populated, still isn't for that matter, but he made it and look what all of us have now. So you see Paw, this is how the country expands and improves. Why, the railroad is coming to Abilene soon, and then the Texas cattle will be shipped east. Someone hast to bring them from Texas now and who better than me and other's like me?"

Brad stopped to take a breath, and his Paw chucked, agreeing that he was hearing a compelling argument.

One evening, a week later, Brad was sitting on the porch beside his maw. He knew she wanted to talk to him, so he took her hand in his and looked into her eyes.

"What is it Maw? You're worried aren't you? Please don't be, Jody and I will be careful, I promise."

"It's not so much your leaving son, I just wonder about your schooling. I know you have done exceptionally well in your figures and reading, but will it be enough for you to find good paying work, when you get back?"

Brad wasn't going to tell his dear mother that he didn't intend on returning to Arizona. He had bigger plans. He didn't want to distress her at this time. He would write and make sure she knew he was safe, as and where he would settle.

"Ma, I've given that some thought, but for right now I just want to concentrate on my immediate future. There will still be plenty of time later for more schoolin` okay?" He leaned over and kissed her on the cheek, giving her a reassuring hug before going back inside.

Maw stayed sitting for a long time after Brad went inside. She sensed he wouldn't be returning and it hurt her heart. He was her youngest, and it seemed he was the hardest to see leave home.

Sighing, she picked up her basket of knitting and made her way back into the house. She fought back the tears that tried to fill her eyes, telling herself not to be an old fool. After all, they would all be leaving sooner or later, and she felt lucky that the girls had stayed so close.

CHAPTER TWENTY NINE

It was the last week in May, 1865 when Brad saddled his horse. With his fully outfitted mule, he met up with his friend Jody. Together they headed for Texas and the Goodnight cattle drive.

Riding along, side by side, on the trail towards Texas that first day, Jody turned to Brad and asked, "How long did you say it would take us to get to Texas?"

"I figger` about six weeks or so, depending on the weather and how many miles we make in a day. Let's say we manage to keep at about twenty-five to thirty miles a day, that would give us plenty of time before the deadline in July."

"Twenty or so miles a day will give us time to see a bit of the country on the way, right?"

Brad leaned toward Jody and answered, "I'd say so. Look, I know your folks gave you permission to come with me, but was it really okay?"

"My maw was a bit uneasy but she said that she felt at peace knowing that you were going, and of course she said there would be constant prayers for us."

Brad said with a smile, "Yea, about the same with me, Paw was better with it than my maw. They said that I had been raised to be responsible and that they trusted both of us."

Jody had always admired Brad and looked up to him like a big brother. They had grown up together and had always gotten along famously growing up visiting at one another's ranches; they were like one big extended family. Jody had several brothers, and like Brad, he was also the youngest of the family.

The first two days of travel went quickly for the boys. They camped out near water, making sure their canteens were always filled and the animals rested. Six weeks on the trail would be a long time and they intended on enjoying it. At the same time they were very watchful, after all this was still the home of many Indian tribes.

On their third evening's camp near a rather large creek, to their surprise they found a beaver lodge. "My gosh!" Jody declared, "We sure don't see many of them around! If there were more beaver, you can bet there would be trappers, I'm glad they missed this one."

After setting up camp and getting a fire going, the boys rested near the creek bank and watched to see if the beaver would be out working. The trees along the bank were fairly sparse and it was evident that the animal had helped himself to whatever he needed.

As they sat quietly watching, they heard a rustle in the brush over on the other side of the bank. A small flock of wild turkeys came into sight. Very slowly Brad reached for his rifle; as he took careful aim he fired, bringing down one of the big birds.

"Jody, how about you gathering more wood for our fire while I hustle over there and fetch that bird?"

Later that evening, lying on their blankets, looking up at the stars they recounted the day's events, each feeling contented and happy to be on the road together.

CHAPTER THIRTY

Towns were sparse as they rode over the Arizona desert and grasslands; however there were occasional way stations for stage coaches. One day after about two weeks on the trail they came upon just such a place. The station was good sized with a main building having a corral in back with a couple teams of horses resting there. The barn next to it was large. In a field beyond that, were a few cattle. Off to the side in a small compound, stood a milk cow and a nanny goat. Multiple chickens were pecking the dry dirt around the yard.

Riding around to the side they dismounted, tying their animals to a railing. Walking to the front they found a porch running across the entire face of the building. Stepping up to the porch they walked through an open door. As they entered they saw an old gentleman sitting by a potbellied stove with his feet up on a chair, smoking a pipe.

An old dog began barking at their approach and he immediately got up.

"Welcome, come in and sit a spell. Didn't hear you feller's ride up. Except for the stage, we don't get many visitors around these parts. My name's Jed Ring and I'm the chief operator of this here stage stop."

He offered his hand and both boys stepped forward. "I'm Brad Kellerman and this is Jody Remstead. We're from back around Red Lake; on our way to Texas, and Charles Goodnights cattle drive. They all shook hands and took a seat.

"Well now, you have a ways to go I'd say; yah hungry? I'll tell my missus and she'll fix us up with some vittles right quick."

He got up and disappeared for a minute into a side room. As he reappeared Jed asked, "You fellers traveled far?"

"Not far yet," Brad answered.

"Well I'm not real familiar with these parts. My wife Sue and I were transferred from Colorado down here to keep this station open for a while longer. Seems rail cars will be takin` the place of stage coach traveling l before too long."

Just then Jed's wife appeared from the kitchen. They were introduced to her and she said, "It's nice to have company. Why don't you boys take your animals out to the barn? There's plenty of fresh hay and oats, help yourselves.When you're finished, supper will be ready."

While they unloaded the mule, unsaddled their horses, brushed, watered, and fed them, the afternoon shadows began to creep into the barn. A barn owl let them know he was on watch for any mice that might be scurrying around. Jody felt something brush across his calf and he jumped, Looking down he laughed, "It's a barn cat!" He bent down and scooped it up into his arms. Several kittens came running up. "Ahhh, looking for a handout, hopin` for some milk most likely!" Jody said with a chuckle.

The boys returned to the main house and were motioned towards the table in the middle of the room. Jed's wife, Sue, entered with heaping plates of steak, potatoes, and eggs. Already present was a huge platter of fresh biscuits, butter, and jam, along with a pitcher of milk.

"Wow!" Jody exclaimed. "I ain't had a spread such as this in ages. Thank you Mrs. Ring."

"Goodness sake, you're most welcome. I like cookin` for a hungry man, or two," she said with a twinkle in her eye.

"Aren't you eatin` with us Mrs. Ring?" Brad asked.

"Honey, if I ate like all of you men do, I'd look like one of them cows out yonder," she laughed. "I already ate, so you go on ahead now and enjoy."

The late afternoon was beginning to cool down a little. June was proving to be hot and dry as usual.

After the meal was finished the boys and Jed walked outside. "We have a spring out back, you boys are welcome to take a dip if you'd like. Don't reckon you will get much chance to clean up and cool off in the days ahead."

"I believe your right about that. We'll take you up on that offer!" Brad said with a wide grin. Looking over at Jody he said, "Ready partner?"

"You bet!" came the gleeful reply. With a hoop and a holler they dove into the spring.

Before leaving the station the boys wrote to their folks letting them know how the trip was going and that they were well. Jed assured them he would see that the letters got included in the mail pouch on the next stage.

Waving goodbye they hit the trail again heading towards Texas.

CHAPTER THIRTY ONE

Brad was sitting by their fire one evening looking at the crudely drawn map he and his paw had worked on together. Jody looked over his shoulder, "How we doing so far?"

"Not bad, we've covered about 300 miles and have passed the Apache Reservation."

"How far to the border of Indian Territory?"

"We're almost there, probably around noon tomorrow. When we cross we will need to be very cautious, not all the tribes are friendly."

"Think we'll have trouble?" Jody's voice had a slight quiver in it. "Like I said, we'll need to be watchful. Our horses are well rested, so we'll push ourselves each day. It means making dry camp sometimes, but we knew that before we ever left home, right?"

Jody gave a crooked smile, "It's a bit different, our actually being on the trail. I'm not afraid though, are you?"

"If we aren't a little afraid then we'd be fools. That's what my pa said and I believe him."

"Tonight we can enjoy a nice fire, so bring out that Dutch-oven and let's make ourselves some biscuits."

Jody had already gathered enough wood to keep their camp fire going all evening. They had their coffee pot on a rock at the edge of it. "While we're waiting for the water to boil, I'm going down to the creek and try to catch us some fish." Brad said over his shoulder.

While he was gone, Jody commenced with getting out the flour, salt, and baking powder for the biscuits. He placed the Dutch-oven on another flat rock at one edge of the fire. He then reached over and got the iron frying pan and put it in the fire as well.

"Man, who ever thought I'd be making biscuits and cooking over an open fire 300 miles from home?" Jody mused to himself. He rolled the dough into balls and flattened them somewhat before placing them on the tin plate that went into the oven. He took some bacon and placed it in the frying pan, which was already hot. They still had some potatoes and onions, so he sliced a couple and added them to the frying pan. It smelled delicious and made his stomach rumble.

It wasn't very long before Brad appeared with a string of three nice sized fish. He had stopped long enough to clean them at the creek. "Boy oh boy, who could ask for a better day than this?" Jody exclaimed as he stretched his long legs out beside the fire. "We are two lucky guys." They sat contentedly, sharing their food and thoughts. The up-coming cattle drive was uppermost in their minds.

Long before sunrise they were packed and on the trail, giving them a good start while it was still cool. The sunrise came out in a burst of oranges and yellows, declaring that the boiling hot sun wasn't far behind. They traveled early in the morning, rested in the heat of the day, and start out again in the late afternoon. They kept their eyes open for any shade. The sun grew hotter and the air became breathless.

Everywhere there were small iron-wood trees, brittlebush, tall cacti, barrel cacti, and pincushion cacti that hugged the ground. It was necessary to be very careful that the horses didn't get tangled in a patch and hurt themselves. They watched the ground for badger holes and snakes; there was always something they needed to be on the alert for.

They had been on the trail for a little over three weeks. Late one breezy afternoon, as they were packing up to get back on their way, the western sun suddenly slipped behind a massive cloud bank. Thunderheads moved in and the afternoon became as black as the underside of their coffee pot.

"Holy Cow! What just happened?" Jody exclaimed.

"Looks like we won't be traveling for the rest of this day." Brad said. He quickly got down from his horse, guiding him and the mule back into the stand of trees. "Hurry Jody, we need to get a canvas up!" He had no more spoken when large raindrops descended from the sky, and the wind picked up strong.

By the time they had the canvas secured and unpacked their steeds, both boys were completely soaked.

Crouching under the covering, Jody asked hopefully, “Think we can get a fire started?”

“I seriously doubt it, the wind is getting worse. If we manage to keep this canvas up, THAT will be a miracle.”

Jody was visibly shaken, “What do we do if the wind takes our shelter?” His words sounded faint through the howling wind.

“I guess we’d get even wetter,” came the answer. As they huddled together with blankets over their shoulders the boys each breathed a prayer for safety.

Lightening streaked cross the darken sky; thunder came like a drum-roll. The very earth seemed to shake with its force. The wind tore at the canvas and, though it buckled, it stayed tied to the trees.

“Our horses!” Brad exclaimed as they heard a frightened squeal. He dashed out from under the shelter and went to soothe the animals. He found the mule had broken loose but he hadn’t gone far.

Brad went to him, gently leading him back to the rope line they had strung between two trees. The horses were badly frightened, standing damp and trembling. “I’m sorry we were caught by surprise fellas, just hang in there and it'll all be over soon." He stroked and calmed them.

He returned to where Jody sat huddled under his damp blanket, "Everything okay now?"

"I think they'll be alright. The thunder came so suddenly it unnerved them. The mule broke his rope but he's quiet now. I sure hope the wind dies down soon."

It was a long wet night, sleep coming in short sprits as the storm continued to rage.

Dawn finally broke with a patch of blue sky overhead. It wasn't raining now, but there were still some ominous gray clouds hovering. The west wind brought the feeling of more rain, so they kept their eyes on the sky.

Scurrying around, Jody managed to find enough dry twigs to get a fire started. Putting the coffee pot on seemed to be the most important thing he could think of doing at the moment.

Brad was out tending the stock. He rubbed them down with their blankets and led them out from the clearing into what little sun was showing. There was good grass and he let them graze. Returning to camp and smelling the coffee lifted his sagging spirits.

"Everything still okay with the animals?" Jody asked.

"Ya, they're fine, damp, like us! If the sun stays out for a while we'll all dry out. Hey, thanks for the fire and coffee there partner!"

As they sat drying out, Jody turned to Brad saying, "Guess this is the sort of thing that could happen on the trail drive. We just got a taste of what it will be like ahead of time."

The boys rested in the grove for the next two days drying themselves and their gear out. Game was plentiful. They spotted herds of pronghorns, elk, and deer along the way. Because they were packed for a long trip, large game wouldn't be practical to shoot; therefore it was rabbit and fish for fresh food. Creek banks offered up wild onions and they still had potatoes, bacon, beans, and most importantly, coffee.

CHAPTER THIRTY TWO

After the Civil War, Buffalo Bill slaughtered over 4,000 buffalo for the U.S. Government in order to starve out the natives, and end their way of life.

It was hard on the native tribes being forced to stop hunting. They were fiercely independent and now had to depend on the army for their food supply. They were expected to farm the ground, with little results.

The Southern Arapaho were talking peace with the army. They had been told that thousands were being held on a reservation.

Brad wasn't sure how peaceful the Cheyenne were. It was known that some of the younger braves were not as settled as the Army wanted them to be. A remnant of hostile braves was still giving them some trouble.

The boys were about half way across Indian Territory when they first ran across any sign of Indians.

It was in the fourth week of their trip; they had to abruptly stop in a sparse grove of ironwood trees after spotting an Indian hunting party.

"We must keep the horses quiet. I don't know if we're in trouble or not, but we can't take any chances," Brad whispered to Jody. The boys drew as far back into the trees as they could. They put blankets over the horse's heads in the hopes of keeping them calm and not signaling their presence. They crouched on the ground and held their breaths for what seemed like an eternity. The Indians passed by them.

"That was way too close for comfort," Jody whispered.

"No kidding. I could really sense my maw's prayers just then." Not feeling entirely safe yet, they shifted positions, but stayed where they were.

"Let's stay here for the night; we'll have a cold camp and that way it will give the Indians more time to move further away. Hopefully we'll be safe from detection. Sound like a plan?" Brad asked.

"You bet!"

It seemed like a very long night. When morning came with its blue and cloudless sky, they knew they were in for another hot day.

"How's our water canteens, still full?"

"Yep, only what little we used last night is gone."

Looking at their map, they could see that it was at least a day's ride to the nearest water. "We'd better get on our way. Boy do I pray those Indians aren't camped at the next water hole."

The sighting of the Indian hunting party had unnerved the boys. They were jumpy all day and it affected their horses. It seemed they were more skittish than usual and that sure didn't help their nerves any.

They rode in silence for over an hour. Then Jody leaned over and asked, "Were you scared last night?"

"Of course I was scared," Brad snapped, "We'd been dumb not to be." He looked at Jody, "Sorry, I didn't mean to snap at you."

"That's okay; I just thought I'd ask."

"You're not wishing you'd stayed home are you?"

“Naw`, actually it’s exciting, something to tell the folks about when we get back home.”

“You planin` on going back home when the drive is over?”

Jody was a bit surprised, “Of course, aren’t you?”

“I don’t think so. If I can get on with Goodnight’s crew I want to stay as long as possible. Then I’m thinkin` of heading up north; might even settle in Kansas.”

“Kansas! Why Kansas?”

“Jody, didn’t you ever want to live someplace besides the desert? Be your own man, marrin` and settle down in some plush green valley?”

“I’m only 14! Why would I be thinkin` of stuff like that?”

“Never mind, let’s pick up the pace and hope that watering hole is free of Indians.”

CHAPTER THIRTY THREE

Before the boys reached the water hole they were stunned and a little frightened by a man dressed in buckskin appearing in their path. He was tall, well built, with an angular face, deep brown eyes, and jet black hair; his skin was brown as tanned leather.

The man, seeing their distress put a finger to his chin and mouthed, "Indians."

He motioned for the boys to follow. Turning aside from the trail he headed up into some low hills. Stopping there he motioned for them to dismount. Crawling up a knoll, they peered down at the watering hole. They saw a large party of Indians, but not the same ones that had passed.

"Cheyenne hunting party just watering their ponies," the stranger whispered. "We'll wait until they leave and then go down."

It was a long hot hour before the Indians departed and their little party could descend to the cool shade of the trees.

Turning to the two boys, the stranger put out his hand and introduced himself.

“I’m David Running Wind Bridger*.” (*name made up)

Both boys stepped forward to shake hands with the man who had just saved them from yet another Indian scare and introduced themselves.

Brad looked a little puzzled, “Did you say 'Bridger'?”

“That’s right, and yes I am "The" Jim Bridger’s son.”

“You’ve followed in your famous father’s footsteps then? You’re an Army scout?”

“Yep! But before I say any more, can you two tell me why in tarnation you’re traveling alone through Indian Territory? I know officially there is peace with the Cheyenne, but there are still some hot heads around and you very well might have been scalped if they had caught you.”

Brad told David Bridger of their plans to join the cattle drive with Goodnight. He shared how they had hid when the first Indian party had passed by them.

"I guess for greenhorns you two did pretty well for yourselves." Bridger said.

"Let's set up camp, I could use some grub."

The afternoon was hot and the fellows sat around the water hole after having taken a swim. They listened to Bridger as he shared a few hints of how they could prepare for any skirmish they might encounter with an Indian hunting party.

"If we're going to cook we need to start now, because I don't think it would be advisable to have a fire after dark." Bridger commented. "We don't know for sure just how far that hunting party may be from here. I suspect they have headed back towards the reservation, but we don't need to take any chances."

A meal of bacon, fried potatoes, and coffee was shared as the three sat and visited. "We sure would like hearing more about you and your father," Jody said.

David Bridger smiled, "Let's see, my sister and I are the last two children my father had and that was with his last wife. Our mother was the daughter of a Shoshone Chief named Washakie, her name was Blue Cloud*. (*name made up)

Dad was getting along in years by then, but was still active enough to teach me a great deal of his skills. My sister and I lived mostly in the Shoshone village for the first eleven years of our lives.

"You left the village when you where eleven?"

"Yes, our father sent us both to a mission school back east. It was great for my sister, but I only wanted to return to the frontier.

"Is your father still alive?"

"Yes, in fact he is. He's in his seventies now and living on a farm near Kansas City, Missouri. He has arthritis, rheumatism, and some other health problems."

"It's sad how all the original mountain men, are now either dead or retired."

"That's not how my dad looks at it. He says he's lucky he made it to old age. He should have been scalped, shot, or starved to death years ago; he's lived a full life. Everyone has heard of his exploits as an Army scout, hunter, and guide. How he explored and trapped the Western United

States from 1820-1850. Why, he was one of the first mediators between native tribes and the whites. He really was a real mountain man of his time, and he was just as famous for his tall tales. Want to hear one of his favorite yarns?"

"Sure. We'd love that."

"Okay then; for a chuckle. He supposedly told this one to a group of greenhorns that he was being pursued by one hundred Cheyenne warriors. After being chased for miles, he found himself at the end of a box canyon with the Indians bearing down on him. At this point, he would go silent prompting his listener to ask, "What happened then, Mr. Bridger?" Father would reply, "They killed me of course." He was able to deliver that punch line with a perfectly straight face.

"Ha-ha that was a good one!" Both boys burst out laughing.

Bridger rode with the boys for the remainder of their journey through Indian Territory. His assignment was to watch the Cheyenne and see that they stayed peaceful and that their hunting trips were for food and not scalps. So far, all had gone well and he felt he could go a ways into Texas with the boys.

He never let on, but they had been watched more than once by Indians. Bridger was well known by all the tribes in the area so they were left alone. Had the boys been traveling alone, they might not have been as lucky.

Now that they were well into Texas, Bridger left the boys and headed back to Indian Territory and his assignment for the Army.

Tired and travel weary, Brad and Jody arrived at Horsehead Crossing just before the July deadline. They found a crew of about fifteen men and boys gathered around a chuck wagon. There were some hundred or so horses in the remuda, and at least five thousand long horns and cows milling around. "Welcome boys," one of the men stepped forward, "where you traveling from?"

"Arizona," they replied as they dismounted, "I'm Brad Kellerman and this here is Jody Remstead. We've come to join this cattle drive, if there's a place for us."

"Anyone willing to come that far just to join us is a little crazy from my reckoning. But it shows guts, and you'll need all you've got. My name's Josh Canfield and I'm ramrodin` this here drive. Rest your bones and grab something to eat.

CHAPTER THIRTY FOUR

The boys were walking around getting a feel of the camp when they spotted the chuck wagon. "HOLY COW! Look at the size of that thing," exclaimed Jody.

A young man walked up beside them and said, "Pretty impressive isn't it?"

"You bet, I've never seen anything like it. Where did it come from?"

"It has a story, are you interested?"

"We sure are."

"You see it's like this... Before this here drive was put together, Mr. Goodnight designed and built this chuck wagon. It takes four strong mules to pull it, and everything about it is unique. There is a double floor of seasoned oak, both pitch-sealed so it won't leak. Sides of the box are eighteen inches higher than normal, also pitch-sealed. That water barrel on the right-hand side will hold a two-day's supply of water. Over on the left side is an oversized toolbox big enough to hold a shovel, axe, branding irons, hobbles, extra harness, horseshoes tools, and any extra stuff the cook or hands might need. There are four bentwood bows to support the canvas cover. Now, come around to the back and take a look at the chuck-box, the only one of its kind."

Jody broke in, "A chuck-box?"

"It's like a cook's kitchen cupboard."

"The chuck box is built onto the very rear of the wagon extending about three feet into the wagon and reaching almost to the top of the last canvas-supporting bow. The entire face of the chuck-box is covered with a hinged door. Look, when opened, it swings down with a dangling leg that forms into a proper worktable."

Both the boys were happily impressed about how the drive planned on making sure their cowboys were well fed.

The chuck box itself had a series of compartments and drawers, each designed for a specific purpose. Across the very top of the box are four small closed drawers. Beneath them was a row of three larger ones. Below those drawers, the chuck-box was devoted to open compartments.

Pointing up he explained, "The little drawers across the top are for flour, sugar, beans, dried fruit, and coffee beans. The first two big drawers are for tin cups, plates, and eating tools. The last one is the possible drawer."

Again Jody interrupted, "What's a "possible" drawer?"

The young man gave him an annoyed look, "Give me a minute and I'll tell you."

"Oops, sorry."

"These drawers contain medicine, bandages, scissors, needles and thread; along with anything else cook thinks he might need. Now, the biggest open space on the bottom here is for a sourdough keg. The rest is for a lard bucket, baking soda, salt, molasses, the coffeepots, and a nice jug of whiskey!"

Walking around the wagon he pointed out, "On this side, over the toolbox, is a coffee grinder. There, under the chuck-box is a boot for skillets and Dutch-ovens. Behind the box itself will be an extra wagon wheel, bedrolls, slickers, extra guns and shells, a jar of coal oil, lanterns, a tin of axel grease, plus grain for the team, and the remuda."

Walking back to the chuck box, he continued, "Just a small amount of food is stored here right now, plenty for cook's immediate needs. The bulk of supplies are stored in the wagon box, along with a side of beef, bacon, and some hams."

This time Brad spoke up, "How is it that you know all this? I'll bet no one else could come even close to describing this like you just did."

With a huge grin he said, "I'm the cook's grandson and I'll be on this drive with all of you; names Fred."

"Glad to meet you Fred, we're Jody and Brad. Thanks for all the very interesting information."

"Mind if I ask, how long you been travelin` with your grandpa?"

"I've been doin` this since I was just a little shaver. My folks was havin` a hard time taken care of all us kids, so when Grandpa started cookin` for the cowboys on Mr. Goodnights' ranch, he said I could come live with him ifn` I wanted too."

"Is this the first trail drive you and him been on?"

"The first real big one, yah."

"It's been a good life for you, living with your Grandpa?"

"You bet I love it."

CHAPTER THIRTY FIVE

The Tenth Letter - Jenny

Dear Margaret,

It isn't often that anything real interesting happens in our little town, as you well remember, but something has come about that is truly surprising. I've gone into the café a couple times this past month and who in the world do you suppose I saw sitting with someone? Can't guess? Widow Spriggs!

She and the McGraw girl, Pepper, have been sitting together. You remember my telling you about the girl that was kidnapped and had lost her memory? Well from what I've been told, she is slowly remembering some of her past. I can't imagine what those two would have in common. Margaret, can you ever remember the Widow having lunch with anyone, ever, in all the years we knew her?

Everyone is wondering what's going on, but so far no one has been able to find out anything. I'm pretty sure I actually saw the Widow smiling once. It sure has the town buzzing.

Can't top that for news, so will write more later.

Love to all, Jenny

****

Fifteen year old Nanette McLeod was not an attractive young girl. Her face was very long and narrow with a large nose and lips that were too small. Her dull auburn hair hung straight and looked greasy. Her green eyes were listless. Nothing about her would cause you to especially notice her and that was the way she liked it.

The thoughts that went around and around in her head every day as she trudged through her daily duties were; if they don't notice me, perhaps I'll be left alone.

"The Quarter" as it was called, in New Orleans was filled with streets that were lined with shops. These occupied the street level floors while the next two or three stories up were residences.

Nanette was a servant girl in one of those Creole townhouses with a jewelry shop below.

Mr. and Mrs. John Kellogg and their son Sidney were the owners of the house and the shop. They were well to do and thought of themselves as devote Catholics, but this did not make them a nice family to work for. Mrs.

Kellogg, as she was always addressed by any of the servants, was impossible to please. She hissed her orders at whomever she was addressing at the time.

Standing at strict attention Nanette was being chided; "Haven't I asked you over and over to never come downstairs without a clean apron and hat? My goodness girl you look like you're ready to cry all the time. I can't imagine why you always act so unhappy."

Her mistress put her hands on her hips and continued. "Don't we feed you two meals a day and supply you with a uniform? You have a room of your own, you get to attend church with us every Sunday and then you have the rest of that day off! Not all servants have it so good! You had better just add a smile to that sour face. Go on now." With that she was dismissed.

Nanette turned and went down the great hall to the kitchen where Ines and Kim were working together preparing the next meal. They looked at her warmly, "Now don't you mind what the Mrs. says, you just stay out of her sight and she won't pick on you," Kim came over and gave her a big hug.

In payment for a gambling debt, Nanette's father had indentured his oldest girl into the service of Mr. Kellogg. To pay the debt in full she would work for five years.

Nanette was twelve years old at that time, and she still could not believe that her father could have done this to her. Nanette's mother, though heartbroken, was grateful knowing that at least one of her children wouldn't be going hungry that winter. Experience had taught her that her husband's gambling wouldn't stop.

Nanette had always tried to stay out of the way of her father when she lived at home, and now it was natural for her to stay out of sight as much as possible in this new place. *"Only two more years, I can do that, I really can with Your help Lord."*

Although she didn't call on the Lord much anymore, He had been important to her once. Even now, as unhappy as she felt, He still came to mind.

The worst chore she had was cleaning the Kellogg's son's room. Some mornings Sidney would wait for her to enter and chase her.

“Good morning little Nannies,” he would whisper in her ear while she struggled to get free. “Having a good morning are we?” He would taunt. “Come on, give me a kiss and I’ll let you go.” She fought even harder but dare not make a sound for fear someone would hear, and she would be blamed. She learned that the first time he grabbed her. She had screamed. It was an awful scene. She had been shamed and threatened with a whipping if she ever tried anything like “that” again. All the blame was put on her.

“Who do you think you are young lady?” Mr. Kellogg stood in front of Nanette pointing his finger at her. “Don’t you think for one minute you can get away with making eyes at my son. You mind yourself or you’ll find yourself out on the street and your father will need to send someone else to work off his debt.”

She ran to her room, bitterness growing in her heart as the tears of humiliation flowed.

CHAPTER THIRTY SIX

This morning she went into Sidney's room to clean, she was hurrying to make the bed and tidy up when he suddenly appeared in the doorway.

"Well, well, it seems I got back just in time," laughing, he advanced towards her.

"Please sir, you'll get me into trouble. Why would you want to bother me anyway? You have lots of pretty girls that like your attentions."

"I'll admit you're as ugly as a mud fence, but you sure are looking good in that dress. Every year you look better and better." He reached for her as she dodged under his arm and out of the room.

"Come back little Nan, I won't hurt you, all I want is a little kiss." He laughed as he watched her scurry down the stairs.

With her heart pounding, she burst into the kitchen where Ines was cutting fresh vegetables on a wood board. The girl looked up startled; wiping her hands on her apron she put her arms around the weeping girl.

"Now, now, it can't be all that bad.

Sidney after you again?" Nanette nodded her head. "He tried to grab me. Oh Kim, what am I to do? He won't leave me alone. He doesn't even like me, so why, why won't he leave me alone?"

"He's used to having his own way and you present a challenge to him. I was hoping he would get tired of bothering you, but it looks like he feels he has the right to tease you."

"I don't think he's teasing, I believe he plans on having his way with me some day. I'm so scared."

She stayed in the kitchen as long as she could and then went up to her sparse little room at the very top of the house. Lying on her bed she cried and prayed until the bell rang that summoned her downstairs.

Washing her face and straightening her apron she was thinking, "I hate this house, I hate the Kellogg's, I hate Sidney, and I hate my dad for doing this to me." Someday Lord, and soon, I'll get away from here and never again will I be forced to live in fear. Someday I'll be free and I'll be happy.

The weeks that followed were better in the house because Sidney and his folks were away on an extended holiday. It was unusual for them to be gone because it was the Mardi Gras festival. This celebration was held on the Tuesday before Lent. Even the servants were allowed to take part.

This was the first time Nanette had accepted an invitation to join in the fun, and she was terribly excited! Heading out that morning the streets were already jammed so tight it was hard to press through the mass of bodies. Kim kept a tight hold on Nan's arm and they plunged through the streets to where the parade was already underway. The music was loud and filled the air. Every few blocks there was a new band of some sort. The air was full of cheer, laughter, good smells. Once they reached the "Market," Kim got them both a bowl of gumbo. They found a spot on the grass where they could eat while watching the parade. The floats were enormous and elaborate. Colorfully costumed people threw bright, beautiful, beaded necklaces to the spectators. Kim got up and ran over to snatch up a handful of these beads. “Here,” she handed one long strand to Nan, “keep these as a souvenir of today.”

The day passed by much too quickly. Dusk began to show through the trees and made shadows from the buildings onto the streets as the girls headed back home. Nan asked a question she had wondered about all day, “Kim, can’t we see more floats from our own balcony? They seem to be everywhere.”

“Honey, none of the really big floats can get through into our tiny streets. When we get back, we can still go up on the balcony and watch some of the smaller floats if you would like. I hate to remind you but we still have to prepare an evening meal. The family will be home later and most likely will be bringing guests back with them.”

CHAPTER THIRTY SEVEN

The following year passed without trouble for Nan, as Sidney was away at school again. Once in a while she still had to dodge around Mr. Kellogg, but his wife kept a pretty close eye on him.

Even though Nanette never could have been called attractive, nature had endowed her with a comely figure. All went well until the week of Christmas when Sidney came home from school.

The family was out shopping, Kim and Ines were in the kitchen preparing dinner. Nanette was attending one of the upper bedrooms when she heard the door softly close behind her. Turning around she looked and saw Sidney.

"What are you doing in here?" Nanette began to slowly back away.

He advanced towards her with a wicked smile on his face. As she turned to flee him, he reached out, grabbing her with one hand and putting his other hand over her mouth. She elbowed him as hard as she could in his gut. Wincing, he whirled her around and back handed her in the face. She fell and he leaned over hitting her again and again. She lay still on the floor, unconscious.

He growled under his breath, "You little tease, I've waited long enough, and this time you're not getting away." He picked her up and threw her on the bed, tearing at her clothes.

Nanette woke up, sprawled across the guest bed. Her uniform was torn, and there was blood on the covers. She ached all over and felt nauseated. "My God, what has he done to me?" She slipped to the floor gasping softly. Slowly she made her way to her own room where she vomited. Leaning against the sink she washed her battered face, straightened her tangled hair, and got into bed. As the afternoon shadows began creeping through the window, she wept. She heard the evening bell ring calling her downstairs.

When she came into the kitchen, Kim took one look at her bruised face and black eye and felt pretty sure she knew what had happened; her heart ached for the girl.

Going over to her, Kim wrapped her arms around Nan. She whispered, "Hold on honey." Nan nodded. Taking a large spoon she began stirring a pot that was on the stove, grateful to be kept busy. She never left the kitchen that evening. When anyone came in she simply turned away, busying herself with the dishes.

Later that evening, when the house was quiet, Kim came to Nan's room. Sitting on the edge of her bed she reached over. Pulling Nan into her arms she held her until she had sobbed herself to sleep.

Sidney would again be away at school until the school break in April. Nanette hadn't seen him since that terrible night and prayed she would never have to see him again.

She knew she was pregnant. The fact that she was ill most of the time made her afraid that someone was sure to notice. What was she to do? She had nowhere to go, no support. She didn't even feel like she had the right to pray. What did she do wrong? She was so miserable she could hardly think straight. She couldn't get fired, not now, not yet.

Nanette was so sick she lost weight instead of gaining. In fact, at seven months she hardly showed at all. So when Mrs. Kellogg called her into the study one morning, she wasn't prepared for what she heard. Her employer sat in a large chair and motioned for Nanette to set across from her. She looked sad and actually spoke softly, "Kim told me why you've been so ill, I suppose I should have guessed. My son is spoiled and I can see that I've been way too lenient with him. I thought sending him off to school would solve the problem, but obviously it didn't. Now, since we are Catholic you understand, we feel you must have this baby."

Nanette was stunned, she put her face in her hands and cried, "It wasn't my fault ma'am, honest it wasn't."

"I believe you, so don't cry. It was just a mistake that needs to be taken care of. You will stay here until your time comes. Our personal physician will care for you and no one outside this house need know. I've given this a good deal of thought, and we'll need to name a father for the birth certificate."

Mrs. Kellogg got up from her chair and went to the desk. She took out a piece of paper and handed it to Nannette. "This is a marriage certificate; of course you realize it can't be in our name, so I've chosen the name. Your husband will be a sailor, lost at sea, named Jimmy Spriggs. You understand this will be on paper only, but it will give you a fresh start and no one will question you. A young widow with a baby will be accepted anywhere. My cousin in Wheeler, Texas will look after you."

Nanette looked up with a tear stained face. She could hardly take in all that she had just been told. She knew she should feel gratitude for having this "mistake" taken care of, but instead she felt betrayed. She was so worthless that her father gave her away? And now she was to be shoved out of sight, sent away to some unknown stranger?

She determined in her heart right then; I'll make this work, no more crying, I'll have this baby. I'll go to Texas and start a new life for me and my child. No one will ever hurt me, again!

For December it felt so hot and humid; Nanette was uncomfortable and felt miserable. The morning her water broke, she was working in the kitchen with Kim. Going back to her room, Kim went to tell Mrs. Kellogg that it was time to call the Doctor. He had simply been told a servant girl was having a baby. When he asked for the father's name, he was given the name of Jimmy Spriggs.

Being young and flexible, Nanette had an easy birth.

"Baby's name?" the doctor asked.

"My mother's name was Dee, so I'll call her DeeDee." Nanette looked down at the small bundle in her arms. Feeling a surge of love such as she had never know, she vowed, "We'll make it little girl, you and me, we'll make it."

Nanette was sixteen and felt like she was thirty. Thin, worn to a frazzle, and scared, she boarded the bus that took her to Wheeler, Texas and a new beginning for her and DeeDee.

CHAPTER THIRTY EIGHT

Eighteen years had passed since leaving New Orleans; Nanette, now called Widow Spriggs, had made a life for her and DeeDee. She had obtained a job in the local post office shortly after moving to Wheeler, Texas. As the years passed, and proving to be a valuable employee, she had been put in charge of more than one small post office in the state. She and DeeDee had moved several times.

Today her daughter was getting married. While it should have been a happy day, it wasn't, not as far as Nan was concerned. DeeDee was marrying a man that she knew would break her daughter's heart. She also knew that all the reasoning in the world wouldn't detour her from making this mistake. Despite her personal feelings, Nan put on a brave smile. Vows were exchanged in a dingy court room with a judge and a couple of county clerks as witnesses.

The groom was a handsome, smooth talkin` gambler named Marcel duBois. How DeeDee had met him, her mother never knew. One day he was just there. Nan saw that he had completely won her daughter's heart. Bitterness welled up in her heart, for she knew this type of man. They were typical of the men who came to the house in New Orleans; takers, users, always with their hands out wheeling and dealing.

As soon as the wedding vows were over, DeeDee kissed her mother good-bye. She and her new husband headed back to New Orleans and to the river boats where he was going to make his living for them.

Nan returned to her flat where she wept for the years of misery she knew her daughter was in for, and herself as well.

Nan sat in her chair and thought back over the years; she had worked so hard to try and make a good life for the two of them. Her daughter always seemed to want more, craving excitement, and wanting pretty things. Their relationship always seemed to be rocky. DeeDee resented it every time they had to move. She blamed her mother for not staying in any one place for more than a year or two. She could never keep any permanent friends. "We aren't a normal family!" she would yell to her mother. Nan could never figure out just what that meant, for she had done all she could, earning a living, and keeping them together.

Ten years passed by quickly. She still moved often, and any news from DeeDee was a long time in finding her.

She managed to receive an occasional letter telling her of their adventures. One letter arrived saying she had a baby girl they named Ruth. There was no further news for over a year. Then two letters came. One told her that her husband had abandoned them. The second was written by DeeDee's landlady saying that she had been very ill and had recently died. Nanette was frantic to find little Ruth. When she made inquires, she learned there had been an adoption.

Nanette thought her heart would break. Her daughter was gone, and now so was her granddaughter. She became ill, losing even more weight, and was hardly able to eat or work. This went on for almost two years. In that time, she completely withdrew. She dressed in black, did nothing with her hair and never smiled. Her heart was filled with bitterness over how life had treated her. She was so sour that any friends she might have had shied away. She was 46 years old and looked like she was ninety.

It was at this time in her life that she was permanently transferred to a new post office in a town called Willow Creek, in Kansas.

CHAPTER THIRTY NINE

The Eleventh Letter - Mary Louise

Dear Mother Margaret,

Our hearts were broken when you wrote and told us about Paw's passing. I know how much you two loved each other. I'm glad you're living with Sissy and her family; it's not good to be alone.

Little Peter is growing so fast. Caleb suggested that we might want another little ray of sunshine to keep him company. I told your son any ray of sunshine needed to come from the sky. He laughed, but I wasn't kidding. I'm not my maw in wanting an entire work crew of my own. One little one is enough, for right now anyway.

The town is really buzzing over the unbelievable change in our towns resident Witch (oops) I mean Widow Spriggs. I'm dying to talk with Jenny or Pam; I believe they know more than any of us about what is going on.

Well it's true, our darling school teacher, Lydia and Doc Hadley are an item. Isn't that exciting, after all these years? Guess the Lord knew when the time was right for them.

Love to everyone,
Mary Louise and Caleb

Lydia stood on the steps of her little cabin behind the school waiting for Rodney to pick her up.

She was still amazed at how the two of them had come to realize their friendship had matured into love.Rod wasn't always able to keep their social appointments because of the constant need for a doctor. Every planned outing was subject to sudden change, but she didn't mind. Today he would make it, she felt sure of it.

Standing there on this warm spring morning, Lydia felt as happy as she could ever remember being. How different from when I first stood on these steps she thought, I was so young and so unsure of what living in this new town would be like. Smiling to herself, her mind went back to the very first day she had arrived.

****

Sitting in the stage coach, she felt parched and tired from the long miles on such hard seats. In addition, there were a thousand questions running through her mind. Will they like me? Where will I live? How many children will I have? On and on the questions went. The stage coach had come to a rolling stop and the door was opened. Her feet no more than touched the ground when several gentleman were there offering their hands and smiling.

"Welcome to Willow Creek, Miss Grayson, I'm Clarence Bellows, the town's mayor and head of the school board." Standing next to him was Carl Rosenberg, who ran the rooming house, and Graham Davis, who has the café. As each introduced themselves she could feel the tension lifting. These people were welcoming her and were happy that she had come. Getting her luggage from the top of the stage, the men took her arm and led her to the shade of the porch that was in front of the general store.

"You must be tired and hungry." Graham said. "Would you like to come over to the café for a cool drink and something to eat before we show you to your new quarters?"

Lydia was immensely relieved and said she would be pleased to accept his invitation.

"We'll take your bags over to your new place and then meet you at the café." With that Carl and Clarence picked up her luggage and headed down the street. Lydia watched them and turning to Graham asking, "I'll have a house right here in town?"

"You bet, Miss Grayson. It's a nice little three room attachment on the back of the school."

Walking up the street they approached a lovely young woman holding the door open. "Welcome," she extended her hand, "I'm Pamela, Graham's wife. And you are the new school teacher, right?"

Smiling, Lydia answered, "Yes, I'm the one."

"Please come in and have a seat while I fix you a cool drink. We are serving stew and cornbread today; would you like some?"

"That sounds wonderful! The food on the trip was a bit hard to digest, what with the bumpy ride and all." She looked a bit self-conscious as she said this.

"I understand completely!"

Later that evening Lydia settled into her new place. There was a small living room, bedroom, and a kitchen. Pretty curtains hung over the kitchen window. There were braided rugs on the floors, a pair of chairs at a small table, and two lanterns, one in the kitchen and one in the living room.

In the bedroom she saw that the bed had been made up with a lovely patchwork quilt. She would find out who had made the fabric items and be sure to thank them. They really made the place feel warm and welcoming.

She walked through a short hallway which connected her to the adjoining school room. This is nice, very nice, she mused to herself. The heat from the stove in the school room will warm my place in the winter; all I need to do is leave my door open. Walking around, she touched the teacher's desk. Looking at the benches the students would sit on, she saw there was a nicely finished long board placed in front of each row for the children to use as a desk.

She was feeling grateful for all the books she had brought with her, it looked like they would be a blessed addition. There was already a small pile of readers that appeared to be for several grades. She took note that there were slates and chalk in a neat pile on one of the shelves. On her desk was a world globe along with a book to keep track of class attendance. In a drawer on the side of the desk there were rulers and pencils. Hanging behind her desk on the wall was a blackboard. She was very pleased to see that the most basic classroom needs were already met.

The following morning she walked over to the café to talk with Pamela. The gentlemen from the school board had answered a lot of her questions the afternoon before, but she still had a few unanswered personal questions.

"Good morning, Lydia," Pamela greeted her as she entered the café "How was the first night in your new home?"

"Just fine! I was very comfortable last night."

"I know the church ladies are planning on getting your kitchen stocked soon. They will be coming by to see what you'll want. Until your cupboards have been filled up, come over here to eat, we'll have a chance to get to know each other."

Lydia sat at the table closest to the kitchen and Pamela brought her some coffee, hot oatmeal, toast, and milk. When she was finished, Pamela had a minute to sit with her as she refilled both their cups.

Leaning close so no one was likely to hear her, Lydia asked Pamela, “Where do I take a bath? Is the privy out back of the school for all the children as well as me?” Her face was pink with embarrassment, wishing she had the foresight to mention these things last night.

Pamela smiled as she whispered back, “Yes, to the last question. As far as a bath, we’ll see that you get a tub for your back porch. You’ll need to take your washing over to the Chinese laundry; it’s located in back of the general store. Most of the towns’ people use them, they are fast and cheap.”

“All this will take a bit of getting used to, but I’m excited about being here. Everyone has been so nice, and the town is just lovely.” Lydia put down her empty coffee cup and began to rise from the table.

“Oh, by the way, before you leave,” Pam began, “I wanted to know if you would like to work here in the café during the weeks when school is closed. It would give you a little extra money and we would love the help."

"Thank you, that sounds great. It will be a good way for me to meet the folks who don't have children in school."

Lydia liked everyone she met in town. The ladies from the church did indeed come and take her shopping. Later there were weekly deliveries of fresh vegetables, eggs, and milk from the various farms. She was told it was all part of the pay required for a teacher, she couldn't be expected to tend a garden and take care of their children at the same time, now could she?

The children quickly grew to love their new teacher. She was very focused and determined to make the best of every day with her students. She was surprised at how easily she adapted to having the first through twelfth grades all in one room.

When school started that fall she had fifteen students. She immediately chose one of the older girls, JoAnn, to help her with the younger students. They quickly settled into a smooth routine. As Thanksgiving approached she showed them how to make stand-up turkeys out of cardboard. In one of the books she had brought there was the Thanksgiving story.

Then it was time for Christmas. Some of the men from one of the ranches brought in a small Christmas tree to the schoolhouse.

For decorations, Lydia let the younger children choose a picture out of the coloring books she had brought, and everyone made long chains with colored paper and paste. A large star was cut out and covered with some glittery paper that one of the parents had donated.

One of the girls brought her doll to school. They wrapped it in a blanket, placing it in a box they had colored to look like a manger. The class worked on a Christmas pageant they would perform during the Christmas morning service at church.

Everyone was thankful that the snows had been light and there had been very little sickness among the children so far this month.

The children drew names for a gift exchange for the "last-day of school" party. They excitedly shared with each other what they received. Also each child had also given Lydia a gift and they clambered for her to share with them; which she did. To complete the party, they had cookies and hot cocoa that parents had prepared for the occasion.

CHAPTER FORTY

"You-Hoo, Merry Christmas!"

Folks waved and greeted Lydia as she crossed the street and entered the general store. She had been invited to a gift exchange on Christmas Eve and she was to bring a small gift, marked for a lady. "What fun," she thought, "But what should I bring?"

"Merry Christmas!" She heard again from Constance Bellows as she greeted her at the front counter, "What may I do for you today Lydia?"

"I've been invited to a Christmas Eve get-together at the rooming house and I have no idea what to bring for my gift, can you help?"

Constance grinned, "You and almost everyone else in town will be going. We're all wondering the same thing. Most of the women will be exchanging something homemade, but you haven't had time to do that, so let's see, what can we find for you?"

They looked at the practical things and the pretty things and finally Lydia said, "I know what I'd like to bring, a box of candy!" So a pretty box filled with mixed pieces of soft candies tied with a shiny red ribbon was fashioned.

"Thanks for helping me with this gift Constance, and I'll see you tonight, right?"

The party that Christmas Eve was the most fun Lydia had ever had. Carl and Sophie were the perfect host and hostess. Sophie had them play a silly game and they caroled along with the piano music. There was a table loaded with finger foods and everyone exchanged gifts. Lydia was delighted when she chose an embroidered dish towel. Her gift of candy was received with a squeal of delight.

Later in the evening she was sitting beside a very good looking young man who turned out to be the town doctor. His name was Rodney, "Doc" Hadley. He arrived just a few months after she had been hired, and they found a good deal to talk about. She shared how she had attended a large Catholic girl's school and he shared how he had put himself through medical college. She mingled all evening for there were so many new people for her to meet.

At the end of the evening however, she found herself being escorted home by this nice young doctor. As they parted ways that evening he left saying, “Hope I see you in church tomorrow.” She thought to herself, “I hope to see you too.”

Christmas morning dawned bright and cold. Her students each had a part in the church service so she had to be over there in time to meet them as they arrived. Feeling confident they knew their parts well, she tried to relax as they presented the Christmas Story to the crowded church. It was fun, and everything went well. The families literally mobbed her afterwards, thanking her for allowing their child to be a part of the special play.

After church, Lydia walked over to Graham and Pamela’s house where she had been invited to spend the day.

At the door she was helped off with her shawl; as she turned around she saw of all people, Rodney Hadley. He gave her warm smile and had quite a twinkle in his eyes.

"What a surprise," she managed to say; praying her joy at seeing him wasn't terribly evident. She glanced over to see Pamela giving her a sly smile. That stinker she thought, but bless you.

The lines from lack of sleep showed on Rodney's face. "I'm just glad to be here, was out till all hours with Mrs. Walters, she delivered a fine boy. They named him David, saying that being born on Christmas Eve he might be a man after God's own heart, like David of the Bible."

"What a special Christmas gift for that family." Then Lydia suggested, "Let's get to the table before you fall asleep."

Lydia would remember the warmth and inner happiness she felt that Christmas day long after it had passed.

CHAPTER FORTY ONE

Lydia enjoyed working at the café during the times that school was closed. She was beginning to recognize most of the town's people as well as the children's parents.

Like most of the single folks in town, she often went to the rooming house on Saturday evenings. There was always music and delightful new folks to meet and visit with.

One evening, as she entered the front door of the rooming house, she was stunned to find herself standing face to face with a friend from her past. "Harley? Harley Thrap? I can hardly believe it."

He advanced towards her, "Why, Miss Grayson, I came to see that you were well. I've thought about you often. When my company asked me to come west for them, I jumped at the chance."

She held out her hand and he took it. They were not sure what to say next, the surprise was so complete on her part and he felt a bit shy.

"Come, there are some comfortable chairs in the alcove." She led the way through the guests and regulars already gathered for the evening's entertainment. Sitting down she patted the seat next to her, "Now Harley, come fill me in."

For the next two hours they sat and visited like the old friends they were. The music played on, but that evening neither one of them paid much attention to it.

Lydia asked, "Are you staying here in the rooming house? How long will you be in town?"

"I don't really know for sure, it depends on what I hear from my home office. I wired them as soon as I got off the train and found out that I had some extra time off. I remembered that you had moved here and I was hoping to meet up with you. I'm eventually on my way to Nevada."

"Will you come to church tomorrow, and then we can have lunch afterwards?" She asked.

"Sounds perfect! It's getting late, can I walk you home?" He stood, offering to help her with her shawl.

Lydia had a hard time sleeping that night. Her thoughts kept her stirred up. Seeing Harley again was such a surprise. They had never been sweethearts, but they had been especially good friends. Once in a while she had wondered about him.

The next morning she found him waiting outside her house ready to walk her to church. She was flattered and yet a bit anxious, what would the congregation think, what would Rodney think? Now why did I wonder what Rodney would think, she mused to herself.

Everyone was anxious to meet her friend. Actually, Lydia enjoyed introducing him to everyone. He was a fine looking man, friendly, and funny. She introduced him to Rodney being carefully to say, “This is an old friend of mine from back home. He’s passing through and stopped to see me.”

It seemed that Harley had more than just a little time to stay in town, for he and Lydia were seen together after school was out every day, for the next two weeks. He rented a buggy and they saw some of the lovely country side together. They stopped for a brief visit with the Wells family one afternoon, and then the Groves brothers another day. Each family shared how they had helped settle the area.

They talked and laughed and renewed their friendship as if no time had passed since they had last seen each other.

Their evenings were spent at the rooming house or the café; perhaps walking around town, or sitting in the town square.

When the time came that he really had to leave, both of them found it hard to say goodbye. She saw him to the train station, hugged, and even kissed him. It seemed like Harley wanted to say something more, but didn't.

"I'll write as soon as I can," he said as he jumped onto the slow moving train, "I'll miss you my dear." And he was gone.

Lydia stood on the platform for some time trying to figure out just how she felt. She didn't think she was in love with Harley, but it had been wonderful seeing him. They had such fun together. Well, she finally decided, I don't need to dwell on that right now, he's gone and who knows when he'll be back.

Time passed. There were one or two letters between them, but nothing seemed to come of it. He had been promoted to top salesman for his company was traveling all over the west, even into Canada. It was almost two years before Harley arrived back in Willow Creek.

As Lydia was working in the café one morning, she looked up and there stood Harley. He grinned and put out his hand.

As she took his hand she exclaimed, "Harley, how good to see you, it's been so long. Come sit down!" Harley stepped aside and beside him was a woman. "Lydia, I'd like you to meet my wife Carolyn."

Lydia was momentarily at a loss for words, and then she smiled and held out her hand." Carolyn, how wonderful to meet you, welcome to Willow Creek."

Carolyn took Lydia's hand and said, "I've heard a lot about you Lydia, Harley told me you and he have been friends for ages. I've been looking forward to meeting you."

Pam appeared from the kitchen and Lydia said "You remember Harley don't you?"

"Yes, I do remember him. It's so nice to see you again." Then she noticed the woman standing next to him. "And...," she hesitated. Carolyn stepped up and said, "I'm Harley's wife, Carolyn."

"Oh, how very nice to meet you." Trying not to fumble for words, Pam asked, "Will you be staying for supper?"

Harley answered, "I do believe we have time for a bite before the train leaves, thank you."

Taking a break, Lydia sat down with Harley and Carolyn and had a nice time catching up. When they left, there were hugs all around.

Pam came out to help clear the table. Looking at Lydia she asked, "That was a surprise, wasn't it? Did you know he was married?"

"He didn't write about it, so no, I had no idea. We were never really more than good friends. I'm happy for them."

That evening sitting alone in her cabin, Lydia thought about the unexpected visit from Harley and the fact that he was now married. She wasn't exactly sad, but there was a lump in her throat when she thought of the sudden change in her relationship with this old friend. Isn't it strange how quickly things can change? *"Well Lord You always know best. I guess he wasn't the one for me."*

Lydia was so busy enjoying her work with the school children that she found Harley never entered her mind again.

CHAPTER FORTY TWO

Two years later

Rod pulled up in front of Lydia's place. Getting down from the buggy he offered his arm to her. As she slipped her hand through his arm, he broke out into a warm smile. "You look lovely," he said as he helped her up to the seat of the buggy. "I do believe it's going to be a perfect day for a drive, and being with you will make it even better."

Rod took Lydia's hand in his when he was settled in the seat next to her. She was glowing from the words he had just spoken to her. "Ready my dear?"

The buggy ride was indeed a pleasant one. The sky was a creamy blue under wisps of white clouds. All around them spring was brightening the fields with their earliest flowers. Wild roses were beginning to bud and tiny bunches of violets peeked out from around low bushes. Getting down from the buggy, they brought their lunch basket and a blanket to a soft grassy area.

Rod led the horse and buggy over to some trees. He took out a canvas bag filled with oats and put it over the horse's head.

Turning back to the grassy area he saw Lydia laying out their lunch. He stopped a minute just to look at her. How beautiful she is he thought, as lovely as the day we first met. Where did those years go anyway? Why didn't we realize our love long before this? Not really having an answer, he walked over and sat on the blanket next to her. Putting his arm around her, he drew her close. They kissed with tenderness. Not with the passion that so often comes with youth, but with such deep understanding it brought tears to his eyes. "Do you know how much I love you my Dear?"

"Oh Rod, I love you too. It almost hurts I love you so much. Do you ever wonder why it took us to long to realize this love?"

He smiled, for he had just been asking himself that same question moments before. He kissed her tenderly again.

"Have you set a date for our wedding yet?" he asked.

“Every bride dreams of a June wedding, so I believe June 10th would be perfect. I’ve talked to Pamela and she’s agreed to be my maid of honor.” Have you spoken to Graham about standing up with you?”

“He said he would be honored. It looks like everyone from around these parts is coming to our wedding. Seems they’ve been waiting for this occasion for quite some time. Do you think they knew something before we did?” Looking at each other, they both burst into laughter.

****

On the frontier, dances, riding, and picnicking weren't the only forms of amusement. The men hunted everything from ducks and geese to deer and buffalo. This might have been for amusement or for food. There were shooting contests in which a woman could compete if she wished. There were horseback races, horseshoe tournaments, and baking contests on the 4th of July and the quilting bees all year round.

In the winter there were sleigh rides and ice skating, taffy pulls in warm kitchens, and group spelling bees at the schoolhouse. Often a literary society would stop through; providing weekly forums for debates, recitations, singing, and dialogues. Amateur theatrical groups presented plays ranging from lively skits to Shakespearean tragedies, giving any aspiring young talent a place to shine.

Settling a new land brings with it hard work, privation, and disappointments. Those who choose to come and stay found ways to bring joy and happiness along with them.

Then there were the children which were particularly valued in the frontier family. Often isolated from distant relatives and past friends, the family was all important.

With their easy laughter, the children bought humor to difficult times; with their energy, they brought lively companionship; with their developing strength, they brought helping hands to the family's labor.

On the whole, families tended to be large. A house full of six to twelve children was not uncommon. The high rate of child mortality on the frontier encouraged many parents to compensate.

On the practical level, each new pair of working hands helped the family achieve greater self-sufficiency.

For children of all ages, the daily workload was both physically demanding and time-consuming. For the younger ones, there were the daily chores of fetching water, gathering buffalo chips for the fires, and picking wild fruit. In later years they joined in the heavier work of plowing and planting, building fences and cabins, trapping small animals, and helping about the house.

For the most part, child labor was divided according to the traditional roles of the sexes. While girls assisted their mothers with the regular household tasks, their brothers farmed the fields with their fathers. These working roles remained flexible, however. When the need arose, the girls, like their mothers, pitched in with the heavy work. Furthermore, during hard times sons and daughters alike often sought employment on neighboring farms or in town.

CHAPTER FORTY THREE

The Twelfth Letter – Jenny

Dearest Margaret,

We just came back from Doc Hadley and Lydia's wedding. It was simply glorious. You would have loved it. Everyone from miles and miles around came. After all Doc has probably treated most of them at one time or another, and Lydia has taught their children all these years. Is there anything more wonderful than seeing two people who really love each other finally getting married?

You asked how I was feeling and all I can say is that Levi and I have slowed down a lot. Levi has sold most of his pigs and only goes to the store a couple times a week now. My leg keeps me humble; after all, I probably should have been completely crippled years ago. The Lord has been good to us.

Emma and Brad want us to move out to the ranch. We are thinking about it. Their boss has offered to give them their own place. They have been living in the big ranch house, but feel it's time to get a place of their own. Will let you know what we decide.

You remember my telling you about the change in Widow Spriggs? Well, all of us have been bowled over watching that sour old widow melt with the loving friendship that Pepper has lavished on her. That's right, Pepper has become Nan's (the widow finally told us her given name) constant companion. You simply wouldn't believe the joy those two radiate. They are together all of the time.

I shall always miss you; you are like a dear little sister. We shared so many good times together here in Willow Creek.

Take care dear.

Love, Jenny

Widow Spriggs was sitting at her usual table complaining about something, as always, when Pepper walked over and sat her tea cup down.

"Who are you and why are you taking the liberty of using my table without my permission?"

"My name is Pepper. You're here alone and so am I, so I thought I'd come join you. I hope you don't mind."

"Mind? Well young lady, I most certainly do mind! You may leave me to my breakfast. I like being alone. Shoo!"

Pepper didn't move. She just sat there and sipped her tea.

"Shoo, didn't you hear me, go away!"

With a twinkle in her eye Pepper said, "You remind me of someone, please tell me your name."

"Why in the world would you want to know that?"

"Except for my paw, I don't know many people in town yet, and I know for a fact that it can get old, always eating alone."

"Oh really! Aren't you the smart one now! Didn't you understand me when I told you, I LIKE eating alone?" Pepper smiled, "Well, if that's the way you really feel, I'll leave you, for now."

Pepper was back the next morning and the next until the Widow Spriggs actually began to look forward to the sweet young nuisance's appearance. This morning Nan had hardly gotten seated when Pepper came bursting into the café. Sitting down at the table, she seemed to be overflowing with a need to share.

"Did you know I was kidnapped on my way here to visit my paw? I was knocked unconscious and lost my memory for a while. Now, I remember being told that I was adopted at about six years old; and that my real mother, Ruth, was adopted also as a young girl. Isn't that a surprising coincidence?" Pepper stopped and took a deep breath.

Nan was a bit overwhelmed but managed to answer, "What? Oh, I suppose so."

"I have some errands that Paw asked me to do, see you tomorrow." and off she dashed.

"Humph… maybe yes, maybe no," the Widow mumbled.

This same exchange went on for several weeks. Despite herself, Nan WAS interested. When she heard the name "Ruth" and "being adopted" she began to wonder. Did she dare think, what if, Oh No! It couldn't be. Still she was beginning to look forward to Pepper's company, even if she kept it to herself.

This morning when Pepper approached the Widow's table Nan greeted her. "Good

Morning," nodding her head as she waved her hand towards an empty chair at her table.

Pepper was surprised at the "cordial" greeting. "Thanks, I'd love to join you."

With a slight smile Nan suddenly blurted out, "So you're remembering more of your past?"

Surprised that she was asked, Pepper said. "Oh yes, my paw continues to tell me more and more. He told me when my adopted ma died; he left me to be raised by his sister. You see, he's a prospector and moves around a lot. He felt it wasn't any life for me. He sent his sister money for my care and wrote me letters through the years.

"Do you know why you were originally put up for adoption?"

"I was told my birth mother was killed in an accident."

"Well, it sounds like you had a hard time when you were young, that I know all about!"

"Did you have a hard time growing up?"

"Let's just say it was distasteful and unpleasant."

"They call you Widow Spriggs, so I guess you were married, what happened to your husband?"

"He was a sailor and was drowned at sea, a long time ago."

"Did you ever have any kids?"

"I had a daughter. I named her DeeDee. Having to move around with my job was hard on her, I can see that now. Anyway, she married a slick gambler, who eventually left her and their new baby."

"Oh how awful. Did she come back home to you with the baby?"

"No, I didn't hear from her for a long time. Finally I did receive a short note informing me I was a grandmother to baby Ruth."

"Ruth? That was my real maw's name. What a small world. Did you try to find them?"

"Of course I did, but it seems she didn't want to be found, at least not by me."

"Is that the reason you always looked so sad?"

Nan looked surprised but answered truthfully, "I guess it might be. You're rather sensitive to others feelings little lady, how come?"

"My maw always told me that too. She said when hard times come to someone at a young age it usually makes them more understanding. She said the Lord had His hand on me."

"Humph! More understanding indeed! The Lord! I haven't given Him a thought in a very long time."

"Why not?"

"Well, it's a long sad story. And one I don't care to share!"

With her usual lack of candor, Pepper persisted. "But surely you don't want to stay sad over something that happened so long ago, do you?"

"Young lady, I believe we've discussed this long enough. Good day!" With that Widow Spriggs got up and left the café.

Pam came into the dining room. She went over to Pepper and put her arm around her.

"I hope I haven't made her mad," Pepper said to Pam.

"I'm so proud of you honey, no one else as ever even tried to get close to that old woman. She has always been so quick to ward off any attempts. I do hope you continue pursuing the friendship."

"Oh I will! I kinda like her."

Pam looked at her with raised eyebrows, "You like her huh? Well good for you honey, she needs someone to see through that rough exterior into her heart, and I believe you're just the one who can do that."

Pepper gave Pam a grateful smile, "Thank you, I sure hope so."

CHAPTER FORTY FOUR

It was a couple days before Widow Spriggs came back to the café. She had been doing a lot of thinking since last talking with Pepper and had decided she wanted to see her again. This little snip of a young lady had stirred something in her heart. It was an emotion she hadn't felt in far too long and she didn't want to lose it. She wasn't sure how to begin reaching out, but knew she wanted to try.

Pepper was delighted to see the Widow that morning. Rushing over to her she blurted out "I'm so sorry if I upset you, please forgive me Widow Spriggs."

"Please, call me Nan." She put her hand out and touched Pepper's. "You have nothing to be sorry for my dear. I have kept myself isolated from friendship for so long I don't really know how to behave anymore. You are correct in saying that I've been sad for too long."

The two of them sat at the table talking for a long time that morning. Once Nan allowed herself to get close to Pepper it was almost as if a dam inside her broke lose she began to soften. One of the first things folks noticed was that her scowl was gone. One day she actually wore a dress that wasn't black. Pepper admired the new look. "Oh Nan, you look so nice. Let me see, what's different?" As she walked around the table Nan's cheeks grew pink.

"That's enough of that, sit down and stop acting silly." However, the usual scolding voice wasn't there and Pepper knew she was pleased.

Pam came in to take their orders, "Good morning you two. Widow Spriggs, you look very lovely today."

"Good grief, all I did was get a new dress." She had a twinkle in her eye however, and a slight smile appeared on her lips.

"Well it's very becoming."

Nan and Pepper began taking walks together after their morning breakfasts. They went to Grizz's cabin and had lunch one day. Pepper shared more of her past as she recalled it, and this encouraged Nan to do the same. They slowly began to piece their pasts together and unravel facts that eventually would lead them to a wonderful surprise; one that would change both their lives forever.

CHAPTER FORTY FIVE

The Thirteenth Letter - Mary Louise

Dearest Mother Margaret,

I write this letter to you with much sorrow in my heart. Jenny asked me to write because she just can't right now. Levi has died. It was quite sudden, seems he had a heart attack. They were working in the meat shop and Levi just fell over. It was quick; Doc said he probably never even knew what hit him.

The town is grieving, we'll be having a service for him this next Sunday. They had been talking about moving in with Emma and Brad anyway, so I expect Jenny will do that now.

It was a hard winter for all of us and we are looking forward to spring.

We continue to thank the Lord for all His tender mercies towards us.

We are especially missing you these days mother, write soon?

Love, Caleb and Mary Louise

Jenny Woods was numb with shock. She just couldn't believe her Levi was gone. Emma sat holding her hand during the church service that Sunday. Brad sat in the pew on the other side of her with the children. Jenny's eyes were dry, for she was cried out. She just felt empty and emotionally drained.

At the close of the service all the guests passed by and offered condolences to the family. Afterwards, everyone moved into the fellowship hall. Tables had been set up with a meal provided by the church's women's auxiliary. Jenny managed to give a weak smile of thanks as she accepted a plate placed in front of her. She was thinking, we had so many good years together. I must not give in to this feeling of helplessness and loneliness. I have the Lord, and a loving family.

****

Standing in the doorway of her home, Jenny heard Emma ask, “Maw, are you ready? We’ve gotten everything packed up. Brad and some of the hands from the ranch have the wagon outside.”

Emma took Jenny’s hand and guided her to the buckboard. Looking back Jenny said, “It just doesn’t seem possible; I’ve lived here in this house ever since we moved here, now everything has changed. Oh! Emma I’m so grateful to have you. I don’t know what I would do without you.”

“Maw what would I have done without you and Paw? I was an orphan and you took me in, provided for me and loved me. You became my family and now it’s my turn to provide for you. The Lord tells us to take care of each other and I am grateful for the opportunity to be giving back to you. The children are wild with joy over having their Nana coming to live with them.”

Once settled in the large downstairs bedroom at Emma’s, Jenny began to fit into the routine of the ranch. Being around the children helped motivate her; they loved joining her for walks. No one seemed to mind that she easily ran out of breath. Their maw was always busy, so having their nana to give them extra attention was something each of them treasured.

The first year after losing Levi was the hardest for Jenny. The first anniversary hurt so much that she stayed in her room most of the day thinking and praying. His first missed birthday, and the holidays, they were the most difficult of all. But as spring advanced, she felt new life entering her spirit; much like the land around her was budding out with new growth, new colors, and fragrances.

Holding on to her faith she knew that everything had a way of working out and she would be able to move on with her life. Jenny found that she loved living on the ranch. There were always chores she was able to help with, and it made her feel useful. Most of all she loved the children. She and Emma had always been best friends and living together had worked out well for everyone.

CHAPTER FORTY SIX

The Fourteenth Letter – Jenny

Dearest Margaret,

Life rolls on and so do we. Days without Levi are still hard. Having lost your Joseph I know that you understand. Aren't we fortunate to have our daughters and family to help us over the rough times?

I'm really trying to make the changes gracefully. As I've often said, and never with so much meaning, I don't know how anyone makes it without our Lord's help.

I'm glad the spring days are beginning to lengthen and the world is coming alive again after the winter's deathly chill. Seeing buds and blossoms on the trees; crocuses, and snowdrops pushing their way through the cold damp earth, lifts my weary soul.

It's fun going on walks with the children. It's been a long time since I really looked at a rock or a leaf through a child's eyes. Seems getting old has its compensations.

Oh! The other night we had the most interesting guest for dinner. An old man, a friend of Josh Canfield, named Harry Cummings. He was a scout with the US Army 3rd Cavalry Regiment at

Fort Robinson back in 1878. He shared such exciting stories of his adventures with us.

Thanks for listening to me dear friend.

Love, Jenny

Late one evening all of the adults were sitting around the fireplace in the main ranch house. Josh's old friend Harry Cummings had met everyone upon his arrival a couple of days earlier. Brad and Emma and Jenny had come over for dinner, leaving the children with the housekeeper.

Harry was asked to share some of his experiences as an Army scout.

"Well sir, I guess I'll start by saying there was a time in my life, while in the service of my country, that I regret having been a part of it. I don't usually talk about any of the ugly times, but tonight I believe I'll share some hard truths with you folks."

He began, "Jenny, you and your friends in Willow Creek must have felt the anxiety. During those years when the Cheyenne hit the western part of Kansas? The killing and stealing raids made an impact on everyone in the region."

Jenny, nodded, "I do indeed remember. We had a few really nervous weeks in 1877."

Harry continued, "In the aftermath of the Great Sioux War of that time, the Northern Cheyenne surrendered to the U.S. Army. A treaty was drawn up in which the tribes would be allowed to remain in their homeland of Nebraska."

There was an edge of dismay in Harry's voice as he said, "As it happened in our dealings with the Indians, we broke every treaty we ever had with them. And this one was no exception.

The Northern Cheyenne tribes, almost a thousand strong, were forced from their homeland and herded off to the Indian Territory; this was to later become New Mexico. They were put on the Darlington Agency reservation, along with their kinsmen, the Southern Cheyenne.

Furthermore, they were told upon signing the treaty that if they didn't fare well in the new territory, they could return to Nebraska. It quickly became apparent that this new place was not a good one for them.

They requested that they return north; their request was denied."

Harry looked around at the group and explained, "You must understand that we didn't know much about the tribes, their culture, or their beliefs. The Army just rode roughshod over them, mostly in ignorance.

There was the Army way, and that was strictly by the book. Thing is, the book didn't tell us how to handle these people, and I believe we did it all wrong.

The northern tribes did not do well in an area that was so different from what they were used to, the heat was unbearable to them, and the air was filled with dust and mosquitoes. Reservation life was killing them, literally killing them!

Most of their horses were taken away from them as well as any weapons they had. Chief Little Wolf and his brother Chief Dull Knife were leaders of the northern tribes. They soon discovered that there had been a massive food shortage even before they arrived.

There wasn't enough game left to supplement the meager supplies they were given for the thousands of Indians on this reservation. The rations that did arrive were wholly inadequate for the people.

In late summer the northern tribes began to come down with fevers, shaking chills, and aching bones. Combined with the fact that there had been little nourishing food, many began to die.

There was a doctor assigned to the camp, but he wasn't even given enough quinine to alleviate the malaria. To add to their misery, a measles epidemic struck the children.

There were some officers who sympathized with the Indians, but their hands were tied. They could do nothing without permission from Washington. The men back in the capitol either had no idea of the suffering these people were enduring or they just didn't care."

Harry stopped talking for a few minutes being deep in thought. Finally he continued. "Within that first year, after being starved, ravaged by disease and death, the northern tribes knew they couldn't stay there any longer and survive."

CHAPTER FORTY SEVEN

The two Cheyenne chiefs met with the Indian agent and asked, once again, for permission to go back north. He told them he couldn't give that permission and that they needed to stay for one more year. The agent promised to help make conditions better for them. The Chiefs refused, saying that in another year they would all be dead. They told the agent that they were going to leave anyway and they wanted no bloodshed.

In early September of 1877, 353 Cheyenne packed up and were ready to leave. Under the cover of darkness they snuck away, leaving their tepees standing empty behind them, giving them added time for escape before the Army discovered they were gone. They only had a few horses so they took turns riding and walking.

After only twenty years of the white man taking over their lands, these people were nearly as scarce as the buffalo."

Harry interjected into his story, "I talked with many officers in different Forts, and later with Dull Knife himself about what happened to him and his people after they left the reservation.

The army pursued the escaping Indians for over a month. Chief Little Wolf and Chief Dull Knife skillfully maneuvered through the western prairies, keeping under cover.

The two chiefs instructed their people that they were to steal horses and supplies from all the ranches, but they were not to kill.

But as often happens in any group of people, there were always those who disobey their leader's orders.

The bloodshed that occurred as they passed through Kansas was horrid. The two chiefs were not responsible for any of that. It was later proven that just one renegade Cheyenne Indian, Black Coyote, and his followers were solely responsible.

After crossing the Platte River in Nebraska, the two chiefs went separate ways. Chief Little Wolf headed to Canada while Chief Dull Knife led his people into the Dakota Territory. Dull Knife and his 150 followers, were caught by an army patrol and in October 1878. They were held at Fort Robinson while waiting for the government to decide their fate.

I was in the 3rd regiment at the time, and that is how I became aquatinted with Chief Dull Knife. He told me then that he was an old man and wanted to live out his days in peace, his fighting days were over.

The commander of the Fort came one day and related that he had received word from Washington. Dull Knife and his people were to return to the southern reservation.

They were told that immediate preparations were to be started, even though it was the middle of winter.

I remember Chief Dull Knife's words as if it were yesterday; "Does the Great White Father want us to die? If so, we will die right here. We will not go back!"

In trying to force them to move, the soldiers were ordered to treat them far more harshly than they had before. Tribes were confined to the barracks and refused rations and wood for heat. It was unfair and many of us felt bad for these gentle people. All they wanted was to live their lives in peace.

Was it any surprise that most of them broke out windows in the barracks to escape the fort? Without weapons or food, it wasn't long before most of them were recaptured.

Still, 38 Cheyenne escaped and the Army was told to pursue them."

Harry faltered here; with tears in his eyes he continued, "Two weeks after the escape, the Army cornered the remaining band members above the Hat Creek bluffs, about thirty five miles northwest of Fort Robinson. I was ashamed then, and am ashamed to this day about what happened to those innocents.

Twenty-four Indian men and fourteen women and children prepared to defend their position in a dry creek bed. Our commander led four companies of soldiers, about 150 men, to attack the position from three directions. Can you believe it? 150 men!" Harry raised his voice with anger and disgust, "We slaughtered those poor people, shot them down like rats in a trap. The dry creek bed later became known as "The Pit"."

"Why do you say "We" Harry? I thought you were just a scout."

"I was ordered to go along with that company. Although I didn't do any of the actual shooting myself, I didn't do anything to stop it neither."

There was a long silence before he continued. “It wasn’t the only shameful act that our Army took part in and it will always be blight on this countries record. I just pray God forgives us, for I’ve had a hard time forgiving myself.”

Harry looked at us and saw the shock on our faces. “Sorry folks, I believe we all need to know of some of the shameful acts our God fearing country is responsible for.”

Continuing, Harry said, “I’m not overlooking the damage done by the natives in the wars over the lands, but I must say that the Indians I came to know, simply were NOT the savage killers some would have you believe they were.”

Josh got up from his chair and placed his hand on his old friends shoulder, “It’s good to share sometimes Harry, what we bottle up inside can eat away at us.”

“I believe we need to pray.” Josh bowed his head. *"Dear Lord, we come to You this evening with heavy hearts. You know what it took to tame this new land and all the wrongs that were done on both sides. We pray for restoration in the hearts of Your people and healing for our land. Thank You, Amen."*

CHAPTER FORTY EIGHT

The next morning dawned sunny and bright. Soft white clouds billowed over a clear blue sky. Returning from his morning choirs, Brad came in with a smile, "Good morning my dear wife, did you sleep well?" He was always so cheerful in the morning. So was Emma usually, but today she felt a bit down.

"I couldn't get what Harry shared with us out of my mind.
I've heard stories of how badly the Indians were treated but it suddenly became so very real."

"I know, I thought about it all this morning too."

"Brad, did you see the anguish on Harry's face as he was talking? My heart went out not only to him but for the Indian's as well."

"Honey, you can bet there are people on both sides with horrifying stories. I hope those times are pretty much past now. There's enough to worry about just trying to survive the here and now!"

Emma waited before approaching Harry. She had some questions.

The moment she had been waiting for presented itself one morning few days later. She was out gathering eggs when she saw Harry out for his usual midmorning stroll.

"Good morning Harry," Emma called. He stopped and looked around in surprise.

"Why, good morning to you Emma, you're up mighty early gathering eggs."

"I like to take advantage of these early hours to seek the Lord. It seems I need Him more and more." Emma hesitated a moment then continued. "Harry, I have been thinking about what you shared the other evening. Can I ask you a question about your friend, Chief Dull Knife?"

Harry left the path he was on and came over to where Emma was, "Why, yes, what is it you want to know?"

Emma began, "Did you know Dull Knife's family personally? Did he and his family die during that episode at Fort Robinson?"

"I did get to know Dull Knife while we were both at Fort Robinson. Neither he nor any of his family members died in that ruckus. I learned later that he lived another six years and was buried at his birthplace in Rosebud River, Montana territory."

Stopping to remember; Harry went on, "There was a fitting tribute to him; telling of his wisdom, intelligence, and courage in battle. There was no condemnation for what some of his people did."

"What about his brother Chief Little Wolf?"

"Let's see, if I'm remembering correctly, he settled up on the Tongue River Indian Reservation. I don't recall how old he was, but I do know he was revered as a great man also."

"Thank you Harry, I'm going to look forward to more of your stories." She stood on the porch watching as he resumed his walk.

Humming, she picked up her egg basket and went into the kitchen.

CHAPTER FORTY NINE

The Fifteenth Letter - Mary Louise

Dearest Mother Margaret,

It's been a very long and hot summer. The crops are suffering from lack of water. We look to the skies each morning hoping to see a cloud, but nothing so far. We have had such good fortune with the weather these past few years.

My brother Gene has returned from college and is working with Sam at the newspaper office this summer. He is courting none other than Pepper McGraw. Do you remember her, the one that had been kidnapped? Well her memory is almost completely restored! She views Gene and Matt as her heroes!

I received a short note from

Jenny the other day. Seems she and Emma have been taking care of an outbreak of some sickness out at the ranch. She said she would tell me all about it when she sees me next.
Love, Caleb and Mary Louise

A small village of field hands on the Canfield ranch had an outbreak of malaria. These men and woman took care of the fields, gardens, and smaller live stock.

When Emma learned of this, she went down to see how serious it was.

She enlisted her mother Jenny's help when they discovered that the malaria was wide spread throughout the camp.

"Mom," Emma asks, "It looks like we're a team again. Those poor folks need our nursing skills. Are you up to what may well be an extended case?"

"I'll certainly give it my best dear. What do we need in the way of supplies, do you know?"

"I think we'll only know that after we reach the village."

The two women traveled the short distance from their home to the village every morning, often staying all day. They saw to the setting up of a central area where a kettle of hot soup was always available. Appetites were very low, but they insisted everyone eat what they could for it was important to keep up their strength.

They stayed busy for weeks, taking care of the sick, cleaning living quarters, and segregating those who were the worst, in an effort to keep the illness from spreading to others.

Josh Canfield was good enough to see that beef was provided for the soup. "Is there anything I can bring down?" he asked one day.

"We're so very grateful for the meat Josh. And since you've asked; we could use some more blankets, tea, and dry mustard." Emma looked to her maw, "Anything else you can think of?"

"I believe you've covered it for now dear."

Two of the largest out buildings were taken over and filled with makeshift beds. As each new case developed, the patients were bedded in one of the two shacks. When yet another group of the field hands were stricken, a third shack was required. Over all the men seemed to fare better in recovery than the women and children did.

Emma and Jenny worked to stem the disease from spreading. One day they were comparing notes. “The sickest women are cold, clammy, and turning yellow. I don’t know if it’s the diet or the hard work, or having so many children, but the women seem to be the most susceptible to this horrid fever. The men are heartier, but still, we have four that are in a severely weakened condition.”

“All the children that haven’t gotten sick have been isolated to a separate cabin,” Jenny said. “They are being cared for by some of the healthy women.”

Upon the outbreak of the fever, word was sent to Doc Hadley in town. They asked if he knew what might have triggered the outbreak. He sent word back that malaria fever and yellow fever were both caused by mosquito bites. They should look for any stagnant ponds or waste piles that might be breeding places.

He also said that if it's malaria, it is very contagious. The illness passes from your hands one to another. If it's yellow fever, a person is only infected by the actual mosquito's bite. It doesn't spread from one person to another person. Since you suspect this might be more serious than you first thought, check with the newest workers that have arrived out on the ranch. Find out just where they came from and look carefully through their belongings. It would only take a few mosquitoes to cause a yellow fever outbreak.

Upon receiving this information, Josh Canfield sent out men to find any sources that could be breeding grounds for the mosquitoes.

There was a thorough search of the new worker's belongings. To their surprise, they did find a nest of mosquitoes in one old suitcase. They immediately burned the suitcase and everything in it.

It was necessary for them to take a new look at the sick and try to determine if any of them had contacted yellow fever.

Josh came to the edge of the worker's village to talk to Emma. She told him, "Right now the most important thing we can do is to keep the news of the fever contained to the ranch. We aren't sure just what we have on our hands yet and we don't want to start a panic."

He agreed, saying that he had already issued orders to this affect, to all his hands.

Not realizing it was dangerous to play down at the creek with it being so low, the children had been bitten over and over. The bugs buzzed all through the village and were only thought of as a nuisance, certainly not dangerous.

The summer had been long and hot; it was no surprise that the men found several small stagnant breeding holes in the nearly dried up creek. They proceeded to clear the ponds out to help the creek to run freely again.

"This is easier than digging post holes," one of the cowboys joked as they were clearing along the creek banks.

"Ya`, lots cooler too," another laughed as he reached down and splashed water on the fellow next to him.

"Hey, I already had my weekly bath! Don't need to be soaked again!" And so the men worked through the days cleaning up the mosquito infested areas. Only the healthiest men were assigned to this clean up. They were careful to wear gloves, long sleeves and a hat with netting attached.

The village had an area where they dumped their garbage. They had been careless in covering it, so this too was an infested area. A very large hole was dug and the existing pile was then transferred into the fresh hole, sprinkled with lye, and completely covered with soil.

Emma and Jenny were thankful to have plenty of water and rags. They applied mustard packs to the chests of those who were down with chills. The packs induced sweating and thus reduced their chills. As the patients began to improve, they were given tea to sip. The soup was eaten by those who could hold down something a bit more substantial.

Emma and Jenny had been careful to keep their skin completely covered. They had plastered flour paste all over the back of their necks, arms, and faces.

By the end of the second week there were no new cases. They had lost three women, two children, and one old man. The cowboys had been busy digging graves in a field especially marked out for this purpose.

One morning Josh and several of his men stood by one of the new graves. "I sure never thought the ranch would be needin` such a large graveyard. I pray to God that this never happens again."

It was still another two weeks before the survivors were up and on their feet. Emma and Jenny were exhausted, and extremely grateful that the worst was over.

Emma, who was sitting outside one of the shacks, turned to her maw with a weak smile, "My children won't even know me, we've been gone so long. Maw, how would I ever have gotten through this without you by my side? I love you so much and am so thankful for you."

Jenny sat down beside her daughter, taking her hand. *"Dear Lord, Thank You for being with us during this terrible ordeal. Be with all those who lost loved ones, and strengthen them as they begin rebuilding of their lives. Thank You for giving us the strength we needed to help these wonderful people. Amen."*

CHAPTER FIFTY

Bonnie put down the last letter from the pile she had brought up to her room. She sat in her chair putting her head back on the rest and thinking about all she had read over the summer.

She couldn't put it into words, but somehow, deep in her soul she felt connected to all the wonderful people who had been a part of her gram's life all those years ago.

She got up and readied herself for bed. Slipping under the covers, she fell into a dream-like state. It was a perfect summer day in Willow Creek; walking down its boarded sidewalks hand in hand with her grams, waving to Sheriff Jeff as he headed for the jail house, and to Mayor Bellows ascending the court house stairs. Doc Hadley and Lydia passed by in his buggy. Looking into the café, she saw Pepper and Widow Spriggs enjoying a cup of tea together. Poking their heads into the general store they said 'Hello' to Constance, and then on towards the rooming house. Passing by the church, there was Father O'Malley pulling the rope that sounded the church bell.

Dream on my Bonnie girl, it really was special being a part of the town of Willow Creek, Kansas.

The End?

REFERENCES

The Homesman
by Glendon Swarthout

The Awakening
by Kate Chopin

Everyday Life in the 1800's
by Marc McCutcheon

Bury My Heart at Wounded Knee
by Dee Brown

The Trail Drive series
by Ralph Campton

The Fighting Cheyennes
by George Bird Grinnell

Mackenzies Last Fight with the Cheyenne
by Bouke
Courtesy of California State University, Sacramento.

In Dull Knife's Wake
by Vernon R. Maddux
Courtesy of Calif. State University, Fresno

Fort Robinson Massacre – Wikipedia

Northern Cheyenne Exodus – Wikipedia

Made in the USA
Columbia, SC
07 August 2019